A marked mage
Touched by chaos
Fights a war to change history

CHAMPION MAGE

10TH ANNIVERSARY EDITION

SAGA OF THE GOD-TOUCHED MAGE
BOOK TWO

RON COLLINS

SKYFOX
PUBLISHING
Fantasy

SAGA OF THE GOD-TOUCHED MAGE

CHAMPION MAGE

2

AWARD-WINNING BESTSELLING AUTHOR

RON COLLINS

The Saga of the God-Touched Mage
10th Anniversary Edition
includes

Apprentice Mage
Rogue Mage
Champion Mage
God Mage

Skyfox Publishing
353 E. Bonneville Ave
Las Vegas, NV. 89101

ISBN-13: 978-1-941676-85-1 (Digital)
ISBN-10: 1-946176-85-0 (Digital)
ISBN-13: 978–1941676-86-8 (Trade Paperback)
ISBN-10: 1-9467176-86-9 (Trade Paperback)
ISBN-13: 978-1-941676-87-5 (Hardcover)
ISBN-10: 1-9467176-87-7 (Hardcover)
ISBN-13: 978-1-941676-95-0 (Special Edition)
ISBN-10: 1-9467176-95-8 (Special Edition)

FOREWORD: WHO ARE YOU?

In the foreword to the first book of this 10th Anniversary Edition of Saga of the God-Touched Mage, I referenced the old rock group Ten Years After. As I prepared to work through this volume, I was struck with the phrase "Who Are You?"

Which made me think back to the days when me and my friends would sit in the basement and spin LPs while playing games or talking about girls. Or while air guitaring, but really, the less said about that, the better.

This was the section of the book that was perhaps hardest to write. First off, a lot happens in the two volumes I'm putting together here. So there were threads to manage. And then we have Garrick finally accepting his basic fate, which means that he now needs to figure out who he is. Even if he doesn't realize that's what he's doing. That meant, of course, that I had to figure that out too. I would love to say that all my characters spring into being with fully fleshed out everythings, and that I simply transcribe those everythings down onto the page. Alas, this is not how it works for me.

I would also say that this was the piece that caused me the most difficulty back when I was trying to sell it to traditional publishing of the day. Looking back on it, however, I can say that that problem was more one of narrative arc and commercialism. Meaning, I was trying to wedge this story into three books of somewhat equal size, and I was trying to make those equal sizes something more in the range of 100-120,000 words each (because that was the size and structure of the standard traditionally published fantasy story.

You might note here that *Saga of the God-Touched Mage* is not packaged in that way.

This is because I realized at one point, long after I should have, that the story I'm telling here is not of that structure.

The story arc worked as eight novellas (well enough to become a bestseller!), and it works in this four-book form, too (arguably even better). But it does not work at three books off 100-plu thousand words because the narrative arc isn't balanced in three waves, and even moreso because cutting the whole into three parts would mean I would have had to bloat them up an extra 30% or so of their current size.

Aside: one of my favorite reader reviews said (paraphrasing a bit from memory) "this is what good fantasy is when you take out all the stuff no one wants to read."

I admit I like that aside.

That didn't keep me from trying, though.

I pulled my hair out multiple times as I tried to find a way to get this into that coveted commercial structure. But try as I might, I just couldn't do it. After a while the effort became detrimental, too. I could tell I was harming the story, and that made me unhappy.

So, I set it aside for a bit.

When I came back, I was a more confident writer. Meaning I understood story better, but also that I was more comfortable with the idea that I didn't need to fit a mold. The Indie world had taken some hold, and without the traditional gatekeepers maintaining norm, adventurous writers were using new structures. As soon as I started thinking about Garrick's stories, I realized what the problem was. And as soon as I gave myself the freedom to write to where the stories needed to go, I saw the whole thing fall into place.

The two volumes that have become Rogue Mage need to fit together, you see, or at least the arcs need to play right. This is because these two pieces, when combined, serve as a springboard for Garrick to, yes, discover who he really is. In the trilogy that I and a few editors and agents saw, they would be separate.

So *of course* they didn't really work.

Anyway, I'm enjoying thinking about the path these stories have taken over time. In a lot of ways, they document my growth as a writer. When I started writing them, I didn't know how to write a novel length piece. When I tried making them a trilogy, I didn't understand story well enough to realize why it wasn't working (and, apparently, neither did the editors and agents I was working with). When I saw them as eight parts (well, really seven, but that's a story for another time), they all worked. The arcs played out in satisfying ways, at least. Though readers sometimes complained that they were too short, they liked them. Now that I see them in four parts, I think the arcs run even better.

Still not a trilogy.

Still not 120,000 words apiece.

But good.

And, yes, once I saw the arcs, I found my joy in telling Garrick's story once again.

Writing is certainly like that for me.

It is a joyful thing. A thing that brings satisfaction.

It is who I am, you know? Of all the phases my life has gone through, the one thing that has remained consistent is that writing brings me joy.

I hope that reading *Rogue Mage* brings you as much enjoyment as it brought me while writing it.

Ron Collins

Las Vegas — 2025

For Tim, Mike, Jackie, and Ken. And of course, for Lisa.

MAP OF ADRUIN

PROLOGUE

It was one of Garrick's earliest memories.

He was four, or maybe five. It was before his mother came to Dorfort, so they were living south of the marshlands, down where the air was always wet and where it always smelled of sugar cane and sweat.

Master Unzi, the man who ran the stables, found him and another boy of the house currying the horses. It was not their job to be with the animals that day, but they were tired of scrubbing the floors and taking straw to the guest chambers, so they slipped away to be with the broodmares who Garrick knew were always apprecia-tive of a soft comb along their flanks.

Unzi made them pay the price of three lashes each. Garrick still remembered the whooshing crack of the sapling as it raised welts on his back. But what he remembered more than anything was that when it came time to pull a new stable boy out of the house, Jakob got the call rather than Garrick.

Garrick loved horses, and he wanted that position so badly he would have gladly taken an afternoon's worth of lashes to be given it.

He cried that night.

He buried his head in his mother's side as she ran her fingers through his hair.

"I don't understand," Garrick sobbed. "I curry better than Jakob. And I handle the shoes. And I ... I ..."

His mother sat with him for a very long time. Finally, after Garrick's cheeks dried and he gathered himself together well enough to sit up—though not well enough to meet her gaze—she said: *"You do all of those things better than Jakob, but Jakob is the baron's bastard."*

As if that explained it all.

Which, he supposed, it did.

There was an order to the world, it said. Everyone gets their place, and never shall they step out of line.

And, yet, a month later when Master Unzi needed a boy to help him calm a damaged animal, he called Garrick to the problem, not Jakob. And when he needed help getting one of the mares to eat properly in the later times of her carrying, it was Garrick again that Master Unzi called, not Jakob.

He should have seen it then, Garrick thought.

He should have known.

A man, it seems, has a place that's given, and a place where he belongs.

This memory stayed with him throughout the long night after the battle at Arderveer.

It came as he sat on a desert rock that radiated the day's heat. Darien slept, of course, and the horses stood in silence, grateful for the respite after yesterday's hard service. He recalled the faces of the soldiers and the slaves and the mages who had died in the rocky caves of the desert city, faces of the men and women whose life force now rolled in the nearly endless waves of power that pooled inside him

This memory of his mother struck him with a force as strong as the twin magics he carried inside him. It struck him as he ran his hand over his shoulder, where, if he looked closely enough he could still barely make out the scar that Master Unzi's sapling had left behind.

Yes, he thought.

A man has a place he's given and a place he belongs.

But the two are not always the same.

CHAPTER

ONE

Zutrian Esta tightened his shawl around his shoulders as he tried to find the right words to express his displeasure. He looked into the basin's smooth surface. The face of Yorl Maggore, the Koradictine mage responsible for the Arderveer fiasco looked at him from one section, Ettril Dor-Entfar, the mage superior of the Koradictine order, filled the other.

"So," Zutrian said. "The Torean god-touched mage has escaped."

"That appears to be true, sir," the Koradictine replied.

"Appears to be?" Ettril responded.

Maggore's face fell.

"I apologize for my lack of precision, Lord Superior. Garrick has escaped. The *Lectodinians* reported him dead, so we diverted resources to taking Arderveer—which we accomplished quickly. Somehow, though, Garrick and his companion fought their way out of the tunnels and escaped the *Lectodinian's* net."

"Do not bring Lectodinian magic into this," Zutrian said. "You were commander in charge."

Ettril Dor-Entfar interceded. "Yorl reports only the facts, Zutrian."

"And I have addressed our portion of that failure. I expect the *Koradictines* to take similar action."

Zutrian suppressed a frown. Cara had been a rising mage, but she made an egregious error in Arderveer. He didn't know how she would fare on the dark plane he had banished her to, but it was certain to be an unpleasant existence at best. If she survived, however, she would be a stronger mage for it.

Ettril nodded his understanding. "You are dismissed, Yorl. I will contact you when we are finished."

Yorl Maggore released his link.

The Koradictine superior waited until he was certain they were alone.

"I will discipline my commander in the privacy of our order. On that, I give my word."

Zutrian pursed his lips. Ettril's word, though of little value, was as much as he could ask for.

"It is acceptable."

"What do you suggest we do now?" Ettril said, his eyes narrowing.

Zutrian breathed the nighttime air. It was always cool in the mountains. That was one of the reasons he liked being here in the Vapor Peaks.

"We look for him," he replied.

"I have a better idea," Ettril said.

"Oh?"

"We wait for him."

Zutrian thought for a moment before he realized what the Koradictine was proposing. A reluctant smile crept over his lips. "Yes," he said. "I think that is a very good idea."

"I thought you would."

"But I want a Lectodinian in command this time. "

The discussion lasted long into the evening.

They reviewed logistics and many plans and methods of capture.

There were many compromises but in this question of leadership, Zutrian was steadfast. There would be a Lectodinian mage at the helm when they finally took Garrick down.

He knew the exact man he wanted for the job.

And in the end, he got his way.

TWO

Garrick let Darien sleep longer than he had planned. The orders didn't appear to be pursuing them, and he was glad for the extra time.

It bothered him that the orders had not come after them. He was not fool enough to think that the timing of the orders' attack, just as he and Darien had arrived at Arderveer, was pure coincidence. The orders should be hunting them now, though the lack of activity from their direction made it clear they were not. He didn't like that. It didn't feel right.

To avoid detection, Garrick and Darien had made their camp—consisting of only a small fire with its now burnt-out ash—in a quiet depression in the foothills of the massive Blue Mist Mountains. He sat cross-legged on a rock, thinking about the orders and watching as the sun came over the mountain peaks to paint the Desert of Dust with elements of dun and harsh green.

The new life force inside him twisted and turned.

He had nearly choked the first time he had dealt with so many lives at once. The lives of Sjesko's villagers had played through his thoughts in solid swells and sudden runs. Absorbing them had been like breaking a fresh colt, like roping a whale and riding it to exhaustion. But the life force he had taken from Arderveer's battlegrounds did not swell or run so much as it scrubbed and burned. It stretched his muscles and made him think his skin might burst into flames. It scoured his throat and brought tears to his eyes. He calmed it as best as he could, learning more about it each time the energy rose, and coaxing it down as it fell. He was learning. There had been moments throughout the night when he thought he understood everything about this glut of magic inside him. At one point he even thought he could trace its link backward to a source outside the realm.

Could he follow that link?

What would he find if he did?

What was it like in the realms outside of Adruin itself?

These questions made him think of Braxidane and of other planewalkers.

He didn't want to face them right now, but the questions stuck in the back of his mind like tree pitch.

For each lucid moment there were many more where he struggled. By the time the sun had risen high enough to turn the desert its dusky shades of brown, however, Garrick thought he had finally gained an upper hand.

Only then did he slide off the rock and wake his partner.

"Are you ready, yet?" Garrick said as he prodded Darien with his foot.

"Wha-t?"

Darien rolled over, still groggy.

"I said you sleep like a rock."

Darien groaned, then sat up, squinting into the cloudless sky as he ran his hand through his tangle of dark hair. He gave a catlike stretch.

"Damnation," he said. "I was hoping it was all just a nightmare."

"No, Darien. This is no dream. I'm afraid you're stuck with me again."

Darien glanced toward the underground city of Arderveer. Convinced that none followed, he rose to his feet.

"There's been no movement," Garrick said. "It appears the orders are not mustering a pursuit."

"Or they're just biding their time."

Garrick nodded. "Possibly, but the orders don't seem to be the types to bide time."

Darien rummaged through his knapsack to gather a breakfast.

"You stood guard all night?"

"Guilty," Garrick said. He lifted the small box that contained Viceroy Padiglio's pet. After the chaos of the past few days, it was easy to forget that Garrick and Darien were under contract to deliver the box back to the viceroy as soon as practical. Takril, the now-expired mage of Arderveer, had said it would hatch soon, and that they should protect it well. "I assume we're going to return to Caledena," he said.

"That would be wisest," Darien replied as he chewed a piece of dried venison. "I would prefer the viceroy not put a bounty out for us."

"I think that's the least of our worries."

"Probably fair enough to say."

Darien eyed Garrick with wariness as he chewed.

How much did his friend remember of yesterday? Did he recall that Garrick had saved his life down in the city's deep tunnels? Could he recall how it felt when Garrick poured the very last of his own life force into his friend? Did Darien know that Garrick had reached so deeply into Darien's essence that he had read his friend's entire sense of being, that he had seen the valor in Darien's heart, and had felt the raw need Darien had for respect?

Did he know that Garrick had felt the joy Darien took at simple things like the roll of a dice?

Garrick found it awkward to know this much about somebody else.

How would it feel to be on the other side?

"You're a strange creature, Garrick," Darien finally said. "I *think* you're good to have around, but I admit you scare me to death. I don't know what to think about this whole thing with you and your god-touched mages."

"You sound wise to me, then."

"Hmmm," Darien said. "I think you're holding out on me, though."

"What do you mean?"

"Sunathri said your magic is god-touched, and Takril confirmed it. But I don't know what that means, and ... then we come to yesterday and what you ..." Darien looked out across the desert. "... I see ... I feel ... " he looked at Garrick. "You know what I mean?"

"Yes," Garrick said, and this time he was the one who diverted his gaze. "I know what you mean."

"Don't you think it's time you told me *everything* about this magic of yours?"

"That's a fair request. But I don't know if the orders will leave us alone here for long enough for me to tell it all. I suggest we find water for the horses and get on the road. We can speak of my magic while we travel."

Darien nodded. "That's a deal."

By early afternoon, they were following what Darien called a trail, but what Garrick considered to be mostly a random pattern through the foothills. He was hot, and as each minute passed he became more aggravated with their lack of progress.

Why weren't the orders chasing them? The battle at Arderveer had been hard and bloody. He expected to be hunted, but his life force sensed nothing coming from the desert.

That annoyed him in ways he couldn't fully explain.

He didn't like it. Not one bit.

Garrick wiped sweat from his eyes.

"Where are you leading us?" he asked with more spite in his voice than was called for.

"We'll be there soon," Darien said, peering through a high sun. "You promised to explain your magic to me, though. Seems like now's as good a time as any."

"I thought you might forget about that."

Darien laughed.

Garrick didn't want to talk about it now, but, having seen the true nature of his friend, he knew without doubt that he could trust Darien. And if nothing else came of it, he wanted Darien to understand that there would be times he should stay away from Garrick.

It was a strange feeling—trust.

He wasn't sure he could get used to it.

He examined Darien. His partner guided his horse, scanned the horizon then peered up into the mountainside looking for this hidden pass of his.

"I was trained by Alistair," Garrick started, "a Torean who was killed by the orders."

"I know that."

"What you don't know, though, is that the same night he was killed I found myself in a situation where someone important to me was dying."

"The girl?"

Garrick looked quizzically at Darien.

"You said there was a girl involved some time back."

"Yes," Garrick said, giving a smirk that was a mere curling of one side of his face. "Her name was Arianna."

"What did she look like?"

Garrick grimaced. "Do you want to hear this?"

"I'm sorry. Go ahead."

"Anyway, Arianna was dying, and I needed help to save her. I didn't know what was happening then, but it's clear now that Braxidane—the planewalker—offered me his magic."

Darien gave a low whistle and scratched his jaw.

"I took it, of course. And I used it to give Arianna part of my life force so she could live."

"That's hard to believe."

"Yet it is true. I carry a planewalker's magic. These kinds of things are possible."

"Oh, I can believe that part."

"Then, what's so hard to understand?"

"I can't believe someone with your conceit would give any part of your life for someone else."

Garrick whipped his head around to find Darien smiling brightly at his own joke.

He was so shocked he laughed. It was a sound that felt equal parts strange and good.

"Yes, that is certainly the most surprising thing about this whole situation."

"I'm glad you can laugh about it, Garrick. There is hope for you yet."

"There is that." Garrick hesitated, knowing he was coming to the hardest part of his tale. "Once I had saved her, I discovered that the spell work left a gap inside me. A hunger. Very deep. I discovered then that I needed to take another's life to fill that opening."

For a moment the only sound was the clopping of hooves on hard-packed ground.

"So, you're in a cycle? You steal life force, use it until it's gone, then steal it back again?"

Garrick nodded.

"And how are you today?"

"Filled to the brim and spilling over. Magic is almost too easy."

To prove his point, Garrick waved his hand at the path before them and cast an absentminded spell. A rose plant sprung up, complete with crimson flowers. The plant would die quickly in the desert heat, but now it was fresh and its aroma flavored the air.

"That seems unfair. Did you know you would be in this fix when it all started?"

"Of course not. Though, I suppose I could have thought it out. Actions and consequences," he said with sudden irony that he knew Darien wouldn't understand in the same way he did. "I would have agreed to anything to save her, though."

"It seems an odd coincidence that Alistair was killed the very night of your … adventure. There's got to be something more going on here. The orders are involved somehow, and I'm sure you understand that politics between the orders is more blood than sport. What do you think this means?"

Garrick shrugged. He was unhappy in the heat, and this conversation wasn't helping.

"I don't know. I've been thinking about it all night, but I admit I have no idea how it goes together.

"Add the fact that Braxidane has triggered my first barrier—which means I am now also a full-blooded mage—and you've got a puzzle that's bigger than I can comprehend."

Darien did an actual double-take. "You have a god as a superior?"

"Braxidane is no god."

"What is he, then?"

"He is a planewalker—simple as that, one of the creatures that live in the spaces between the planes. That makes Braxidane powerful, but it does not make him a god."

"Does the difference matter?"

"It does to me."

An awkward silence rose.

Garrick shaded his eyes and scanned for scouts. "Why are they not hunting us?" he said.

"Let's not be upset by good fortune."

Garrick chuckled. He was surprised to find he felt better.

"Regardless of anything else, Darien, this means you need to be careful around me. Braxidane's magic has a will of its own. As my reserves fall, the beast gets hungry. I can calm it now, but after a point I lose control."

"I thought as much."

"What do you mean?"

"Do you think you're particularly cunning about that?"

Garrick reddened with the accusation. "Yet you've stayed around?"

"There is something about you, Garrick. I felt it the moment I met you. Using sorcery at a gaming table is not a normal thing to do."

"I told you, I didn't—"

"Don't lie to me, Garrick. I smelled it. Your spellwork was unmistakable."

"I was healing the man next to me," Garrick snapped.

"Healing?"

"Yes, healing."

Darien broke out in an obnoxious guffaw that dredged up memories of young boys who poked fun at him as they trudged to their studies and he went off to the stables.

"Healing? At a gaming table? You may be a full mage by power, but only an apprentice would be idiotic enough to use magic at a gaming table and *not* try to fix the odds."

"I'm not stupid."

"I'm sorry," Darien said, still grinning.

"You don't know what it's like to be broken, do you, Darien? You don't know what it's like to be without?" His anger spilled over him then, and he let it roll off his lips. "You know exactly who you are. You know who your father is. You know what your brother did. You have an entire history behind you, and yet you despair over something as trivial as whether you will rate against that same brother. But, let me tell you about *not* rating, Darien. Let me tell you about not having anyone to turn to, about growing up away from your mother because your baron owed coins to a sorcerer, or about cleaning stalls, or about not letting yourself grow close to anyone because you're just going to leave again soon."

It felt good to say these things out loud for once.

It felt freeing.

It gave him a new sense of power.

"I'm sorry," Darien said softly. "I didn't know."

"Of course you didn't." Garrick nodded then, gathering himself together as his anger wound down. "It's all right," he said to Darien. "I just needed you to know."

Darien's beard bristled at his chin as he pursed his lips. They rode in silence for several minutes before coming to an opening that led to the opposite side of the range.

"This way," Darien said, pointing.

"About time," Garrick replied.

He wiped his brow and guided his horse to follow his friend into the pass.

THEY EMERGED several hours later on the eastern side of the mountains. It was cooler here, and green everywhere. It smelled of the forest, of peat, leaves, and wet rain. He had forgotten how much he liked the color of trees.

They made camp in a copse of sycamore and elm. Darien built a fire that warmed them, and they cooked the quail that Darien had taken shortly after they stopped. Garrick ate for taste and companionship rather than for hunger, though he had to admit the bird was delicious.

"It feels good to be out of the desert," Garrick said.

Darien nodded.

ON THE OTHER side of the mountain, a rose plant covered itself against the nighttime chill.

A fortnight later, Garrick and Darien came again to the rolling hills at the outskirts of Caledena.

The journey had remained strangely quiet. They discussed this often as they made camps, and Darien had finally talked himself into the position that the orders' appearance at Arderveer had been an action against Takril for some issue both unknown and unknowable to those outside the orders. In other words, he had convinced himself that Garrick and Darien's arrival in Arderveer just as the orders had convened there had to have been the most strange of coincidences.

"No one can be sure of anything that happens behind closed doors," Darien explained. "But as long as everything else is quiet, I guess no one should care."

Garrick didn't argue, but Darien had not seen the damage the orders had done to Alistair's manor, Darien had not seen the inhuman glow in the eyes of his superior after Garrick had so unwisely given the thing its new life, and Darien most definitely did not understand exactly how unusual it was for the Koradictine and Lectodinian sects to have actually banded together. To Darien's mind, histories were full of enemies in one battle merging to face a common foe, then splitting again.

So, no, Darien did not understand that the orders of sorcery had schisms that were sharper than a honed blade and that ran deeper than blood. They would not work together for something as frivolous as the destruction of a single Torean mage—powerful though that Torean might be.

There had to be more.

Neither Darien nor Garrick, however, were going to be upset about it now that they had made their way back to the city.

The passage of spring into summer had turned the surrounding trees bold and green. The breeze blowing currents through knee-high grasses smelled of ragweed and wild strawberry, and the fields outside the city were now tilled and planted. But, as Garrick and Darien entered the city it became clear that Caledena was still the same dog's breath of a town it had always been. Ale houses and gambling rooms still ringed the outskirts of its limits, and its open marketplaces were still chaotic mills of people trading their goods, services, and sometimes their bodies. The streets were as dirty and unkempt as before, tainted by the smells of smithy fires and human refuse.

The people of the city stared at Garrick, whispering and pointing, diverting their glances as he turned to them.

"Your legend precedes you," Darien said.

Garrick sat straighter.

Let them whisper, he thought. It was best they fear him.

He let the essence of his magic flow over the city and found an edgy cacophony of energies, a mix of emotions that were equal parts hate, hope, pain, and joy. It made him anxious. Caledena was a working town full of people who were just trying to hold on as each day trickled by, but Caledena was also a city of dangerous people who were not above taking advantage of situations that might open to them. He struggled to separate one from another.

As they made their way through the city, the leather bag with the viceroy's egg in it weighed against his thigh.

He looked at Darien.

His partner had grown pensive the past few days, more quiet than normal. When he did speak, it was mostly about the politics of Dorfort, the orders, and even about Sunathri and the independent Freeborn House she had created.

Darien liked the idea behind that order.

"It's unlike you to be so quiet," Garrick said as they neared the end of their trip.

Darien ran a hand over his horse's neck.

"What are you going to do now?" he replied.

"Return this box to Hersha Padiglio, collect my payment, and buy this horse."

"I mean after that?"

"You want to know if I intend to join the Freeborn?"

"It seems a practical thing for a Torean to do."

"It's nice to see you're worried about me."

Darien smiled. "After seeing what the orders did in Arderveer, it just seems like the safest bet."

"I thought you were of the mind that says the orders aren't going to be a problem?"

"They'll still be looking for Toreans."

"I'll deal with them soon enough, then. But I see no need to align with the Freeborn to do it."

"You'll be a rogue mage, then? A one-man vigilante?"

"I prefer to call it remaining neutral."

"Typical."

"I don't play well with others."

"Your thinking is shortsighted," Darien said. "Regardless of what the orders do or don't do, your god-touch gives you a destiny. Sunathri seems a good leader, and the Freeborn appears to be a good group. The people could like them, or at least tolerate them better than the orders."

Garrick chuckled. "That will be the day."

"I could even see Dorfort aligning with the Freeborn someday."

"Spoken like the son of a politician."

Darien grumbled.

"You are a true visionary, Darien. But I have enough trouble sorting out my destiny without worrying about the rest of the world."

"Perhaps they are one."

Garrick looped his horse's reins in his hand.

"All I want to do right now is to deliver this egg and get out of the city."

Darien shrugged, and the two turned the corner that would lead them to the viceroy's manor.

"Hold," Garrick said, raising a hand and narrowing his gaze. Something bothered him.

"What is it?" Darien asked.

"I don't know."

He closed his eyes and focused on the essence of the city. He sensed the same brittle edge to Caledena's aura he had felt from a distance.

"Something's different," he finally said.

"I don't notice anything," Darien said.

Kalomar nickered.

Garrick put his hand on the horse's flank. The animal had grown important to him—he was bright and reliable. Garrick trusted Kalomar instinctively, and the horse was worried, too.

Still, he could see nothing wrong.

"Maybe it's nothing," Garrick finally said.

They spurred their horses forward.

Moments later Kalomar pinned his ears back, and Garrick's gaze flashed around the area.

"There are no guards in the street," Darien suddenly said.

Garrick nodded. Now that he had seen that one element, the rest of the pattern fell into place. Broken glass ringed several windows, and ragged parchment flapped from others. The normal throng of street derelicts was suddenly missing.

"We best leave," Garrick said, reaching for his link.

But a wave of Lectodinian sorcery grew suddenly strong, and just as suddenly, Garrick found himself unable to move. He struggled against magical bindings but got nowhere. He let his energy rise, but with his arms and legs locked in place, there was little he could do with them.

Darien, too, had been so restrained.

"Welcome to Caledena," a familiar voice came from behind.

Lectodinian mages came into his view, the leader wearing a loose-fitting tunic with leather drawstrings that dangled to his chest. His hair was short, and a cowlick stood up in the back.

"Elman," Darien said. "I thought we had seen the end of you when you ran away back in the mountains."

Lectodinian mages surrounded them, the strength of their binding spells far greater than the sum of their parts. It reminded Garrick of the magic he had fallen prey to in the depths of Arderveer —that, too, had been the result of many mages working together.

"You've learned to bring numbers," Garrick said to Elman.

"Lectodinians may have a certain vanity about us, but you would be a fool to confuse vanity with weakness, or a lack of intelligence."

Garrick did not reply.

Elman leaned in closer, and the smells of tobacco and lemony magic grew strong.

"Things are a bit different from the last time we met, aren't they, Garrick?"

"We intend you no harm," Garrick replied. "We just want to see the viceroy."

Elman stepped back. An amused smile crossed his face.

"Do you hear that, my friends?" Elman bellowed to his compatriots. "They intend no harm!" He strolled around the ground before Garrick, his elbows spread wide and his chest thrust outward.

The mages around him chuckled with mirth.

"My Torean friend," Elman said, his smile growing bolder. "You are *looking* at the viceroy of Caledena."

Darien's lips thinned.

"You are a fish in my net, Garrick. You struggle and squirm, yet your efforts serve only to entangle you further." Elman turned to the rest of his mages. "We will have a little parade, shall we not? A little celebration to show the people what happens to men who defy our commands."

The mages took their harnesses and paraded the horses toward the manor.

People of Caledena looked out their windows, staring with big eyes and lost faces. It was a fear Garrick knew well, a fear that drove compliance and spoke of understanding one's place.

He glanced at Darien but saw no expression.

They passed the viceroy's manor, and Garrick saw its stone walls were scorched black, and that glass from the windows lay shattered on the ground. Its drapery was torn and tangled and had been left to flutter in the breeze. The gateway leading to the stables was ripped from its place.

How had he missed these signs?

He would learn from this. He had felt discomfort within the city but ignored it. It wouldn't happen again.

Garrick scanned the stables, looking for the boy who had given him care of Kalomar. He was nowhere to be found. If the orders had hurt the boy, Garrick was going to take special joy at this vengeance, whenever it came.

They took him to a mud-brick building that had once been a gambling hall but was now apparently their headquarters. The building was built low to the ground with a row of windows facing outward. Sheets of blue and red fabric draped the outside walls, each marked with Lectodinian triangles and Koradictine flames.

Mages and apprentices stood before the entrance, the expressions on their faces showing exactly how uncomfortable they were with the idea of being too near him.

"Bring them in," Elman said before disappearing into the building.

They took Darien first, then Garrick.

It took two men to pull him from Kalomar. His life force stirred at their touch, but Garrick controlled it with an ease that surprised him.

"Hurt my horse," Garrick said, "and you will each die."

The pouch with the box swung precariously free as the Lectodinians moved him. Several mages worked to carry his rigid frame into a small room that had earlier served as the proprietor's office.

A short table and a businessman's desk sat toward the window. A painting of a nude woman covered one wall, and an over-stuffed bookshelf decorated another. The room smelled of mold and burnt tallow.

They placed Darien at one end of the table, Garrick at the other.

A pair of Lectodinian mages entered the room, sorcerous concentration etched with intensity on their faces. These two were the focal point of the spell that bound them. Garrick tried to remember, but could not tell if they had come from Arderveer or not.

He expected they did.

Other mages filed into the room, their closeness and their numbers were an ostentatious display of power that seemed unnecessary as long as the two critical Lectodinian casters kept their concentration properly focused. That was something that annoyed Garrick about the orders—they thought that image was as important as truth.

Perhaps he could use this to his advantage.

Elman's boots clacked against the wooden floor.

"So," the Lectodinian said, peering down at Garrick as he came to the other side of the table. "What do you think my superiors will think of me when I show them your head?"

Garrick merely raised his eyebrows.

"What's that? You think they will give me a promotion? Why, thank you. You are far too kind." Elman waved a hand in mock humility, then bent low to put his face directly before Garrick's. "I understand we have a mutual acquaintance."

"I'm certain I don't know anyone you know, Elman."

The Lectodinian mage laughed.

"Don't be so quaint, Garrick. Does the name Alistair mean anything to you?"

Garrick's gaze narrowed. "You were there?"

Elman's smile oozed over his face, and he raised a pointed index finger. "Somehow I missed you that time. But I'll not make that same mistake again."

His eyes went to the bag at Garrick's waist.

"What is this?"

The Lectodinian avoided touching him as he untied the thong and held the bag up for all to see.

"I really wouldn't play with that if I were you."

"Thanks so much for the warning," Elman replied.

His voice rose as he untied the bag. "Let's see what we have inside, why don't we?"

The box slid into Elman's palm.

A smile unfolded on his lips.

He placed the box on the desktop and pried open the copper latch. A brown and blue egg sat in a velvet-lined depression.

"Very interesting," Elman said.

He waved his hand over the egg and whispered a few words, preening as the egg glowed with a purple sheen.

"Yes," he said with a cooing tone. "Interesting, indeed. Perhaps your earlier assessment will prove to be correct, Garrick. Perhaps Lord Esta *will* find it in his heart to give me a promotion."

Elman closed the box but did not latch it. He looked Garrick in the eye, and spoke to the rest of the room with a voice that was cold, and even.

"Kill them," he said.

As he spoke, the window across the room exploded inward.

FOUR

A lamp of burning oil flew across the room. Flames spewed over the table and floor before catching on the drapery and running up to the ceiling. Outside, wizards, dressed in black, cast magic, their faces covered with dark kerchiefs.

A rumbling explosion belched from someplace distant.

The mages in the room broke and scattered for cover, and the spell that had bound Garrick so tightly was suddenly gone.

He whirled and cast a bolt of energy at Elman.

The Lectodinian matched his magic, and the two sorceries met with an explosion that rent the air and caused the box with the viceroy's pet inside to skitter across the tabletop.

Elman grabbed for it but missed. The egg slipped out, tumbling to hit the floor with a muted crunch.

A creature crawled from the shell.

It was small and dark, with a slick wetness to it. It smelled of rotten fruit so strong that everyone in the room gagged. The creature splayed itself over the floor, then crouched and shot forward to latch onto a wizard's face.

Darien, wasting no time, grabbed a wizard's sword and swung at the Lectodinian closest to him.

The mage cast green flame, but Darien still managed to skewer him.

"Come on," Darien cried, running to the door.

Garrick followed.

They found themselves outside the mages' headquarters.

Sorcerous fire filled the streets, and the odors of Koradictine magic merged with Lectodinian spellwork. It merged with another aroma, too; the strange and wild flavor of Torean magic that was equal parts bitter and sweet.

Garrick set his gates and cast raw energy at mages, guards, or anything else that moved. Now that he was free, his magic roiled inside him. He felt the entirety of the city as if he was everywhere at the same time.

A black-garbed mage came through an alleyway, then another, both covered head to toe with only their eyes exposed. They moved with catlike grace and militaristic precision, exposing themselves only long enough to cast spells before ducking back to shelter and rushing to new locations.

Toreans, he thought.

Or at least *not* Lectodinians and *not* Koradictines.

Garrick and Darien ran.

Citizens scurried for cover.

A fiery explosion tore through the headquarters and set the Koradictine banner ablaze. An animalistic growl rumbled from inside the building, and a terrified scream ripped the air.

The viceroy's pet was on a rampage.

How quickly would it grow?

How far would its rampage take it?

Garrick's attention was drawn by a Koradictine preparing to attack an unsuspecting Torean. Without conscious thought, Garrick loosed a bolt of pure life force, and the Koradictine quite literally disintegrated.

A black-clad mage motioned them toward an alley.

"Do you want to stay and fight?" Darien asked.

"No," Garrick said.

They ran to the alley and found two of the dark mages waiting with horses.

"Mount up," one said.

Garrick recognized her voice, then her eyes.

"Suni?"

"In the flesh."

"So your friends are?"

"The Freeborn, of course. Get on the damned horse."

"Why am I not surprised?" Garrick said.

"Get your people away from that house," Darien yelled as he mounted. "There's a creature in there. I have no idea exactly what it is, but I'm certain none of us want to be anywhere near it."

Sunathri nodded, then blew a piercing two-toned whistle.

The Toreans fell back in a coordinated retreat.

"Let's go," she said.

"Where's Kalomar?" he asked.

"Who?"

"My horse. I promised I would keep him safe."

"How in the gods' names should I know where a horse is? Now, shut up and get going!"

"It's important to me."

"It's time to go, Garrick," Darien said, leading him toward the horses Sunathri had provided.

As if by its own decision, Garrick's energy rose to scry the city. He sensed fear and confusion—but mostly he felt the cold black essence of Hersha Padiglio's pet in the middle of the headquarters. Just the touch of the creature's aura was enough to make Garrick want to retch. Its strength overpowered everything around it, and he could not discern anything new about the city.

He got no read, however, on Kalomar, and no read on Will, the stable boy.

Garrick grimaced.

Darien was right, they had to leave now. But he would come back after things had settled, and he would find both the horse and the boy if he could.

He mounted up, then dug his heels into the flanks of his horse and hung on as they raced through the streets. Another blood-curdling screech came as they reached the outskirts of town.

The confusion of the moment made their retreat easier than it might otherwise have been.

THEY ENTERED the woods and rode even farther before Sunathri brought them to a halt. With a moment to breathe, Garrick and Darien found there were just five Torean wizards with them.

"Five mages can create such a stir?" Darien said.

Sunathri removed her black wrap. "Surprise can be a powerful advantage if you use it well."

Darien nodded. "And I would say you did just that."

"Not well enough," she said as she turned to Garrick. "We lost two men. I hope you're worth it."

FIVE

The Freeborn moved through the forest like ghosts. They were alert to each wild call, noted each bird that flitted between the branches, and examined each print of a rabbit or doe or creature of prey that crossed over this ground. Darien, too, worked the woods, merging easily with the band of mages.

It left Garrick feeling alone, again. Isolated and out of place.

They arrived at the makeshift camp the Freeborn had pitched at the juncture of two creeks and the Blue River, in a clearing made amid a rugged ring of oak and evergreen trees. A stew pot dangled over a smokeless fire, its aroma rich and tantalizing. The men and women of the Freeborn gathered around as they entered camp, maybe fifty in all. Every one of them looked at Garrick with a sense of expectation that left him feeling naked. These expressions said he had been rescued for a purpose, that after a long fight against over-whelming odds the Freeborn were desperate for hope.

Sunathri dismounted.

"Welcome to our home," she said with thinly disguised sarcasm. "Get some food and we can start planning."

"Thank you," Darien replied.

He and Garrick dismounted and walked toward the kettle.

"You see it, don't you," Darien said.

"See what?"

"The way they look at you."

"Yes, Darien. I see it."

"And?"

"Don't start this again."

His partner's silence was sharp as a blade.

They served themselves at the stewpot. The broth was filled with venison, rabbit, tubers, and wild scallion. The broth boiled at the edges of the pot. They took their bowls to a quiet creek bed and sat down at the root of a large sycamore.

Springtime had turned to summer, but the breeze here was cool and fresh. Water slid over slick stones of brown, red, and orange.

"I'm sorry," Garrick said. "That was uncalled for. I didn't ask for this, though. It's all too much. I'm not ready to be the Torean leader."

"The Freeborn would accept you as Sunathri's champion."

"That's not how it works, and you know it. I'm god-touched. If I join the Freeborn, I'm the leader."

A crooked expression came to Darien's face.

"I see," he said.

"You see what?"

"How could I have missed it before?"

"Missed what?"

"You're probably telling the truth about being afraid to lead, but that's not why you're avoiding the Freeborn. You're ducking this because you're afraid to commit to anything larger than yourself. It's easier for you to just complain about everyone else than it is to do what you think is right."

"Is that what you think?" Garrick replied.

"I see it all over your face."

"We are only a half-day's ride from Dorfort," Garrick said.

"And?"

"Will you go see your father?"

"What does my father have to do with this?"

Garrick scoffed. "How can you can sit there and tell me about *my* inner demons, when you're afraid to deal with your own?"

"My issues with my father are different," Darien said. "Even you can see that. The Freeborn is different."

"You should join them yourself, then."

"I think I will."

Garrick raised an eyebrow. "You're no mage."

"They won't care, and I find their cause just."

"There is no just cause," Garrick said, feeling strange and more than a little annoyed at himself as he once again finished the thought inside his mind, *only actions and consequences.*

"You don't really believe that, do you?"

"I don't know what I believe, Darien. But I know I don't want to rely on anyone, and I don't want anyone relying on me."

Darien's face grew clouded. He stood deliberately, cradling his bowl.

"Tell that to your new superior."

He strode away.

Garrick spooned stew and tried to settle down again. He leaned back against the tree trunk. Darien didn't understand—probably couldn't understand—but, nonetheless, who did he think he was telling Garrick what he should and shouldn't do?

Footsteps rustled behind him.

This time it was Sunathri who sat down, her forearm brushing his. The contact was brief, yet still felt warm, and still felt intimate.

"Caledena is an example of what it will be like if the orders take control."

"Caledena happened because the orders were looking for me. That's all," Garrick said. "That's why our path to the city was so simple. The orders decided to wait in ambush, rather than attack straight away when I might be prepared for them."

"That's true enough as far as it goes, Garrick, but you're missing big parts of the picture and your view is too short-sighted. That the orders were able to take Caledena so easily shows they are capable of doing whatever they want, and that they did take it shows they will continue to do so as soon as it meets their purpose." Her eyes were dark, and her hair hung to her shoulders. She kneaded her temple. "We need you desperately, Garrick. You're god-touched. History is filled with lessons taught by short-sighted people. Don't be one of them."

"I have other things I need to do."

"I know," she said. "You intended to fight the orders on your own."

"Darien's lips are too loose."

"Let me help you. I know where the orders' weaknesses are. I have people in important positions. We can do this together."

Her eyes blazed, then.

He could get lost in the depths of those eyes.

She was attractive in the magnetic way that true leaders are attractive, a way beyond the physical, a way that dug under his skin. But as he looked up at the darkening sky, and as he felt the feather-like tickle of his hunger stir inside him, he was suddenly afraid for her, afraid for what he could do to her if she trusted him too far, and for what, in turn, that would once again do to him.

"It's not a good idea, Suni."

"We can't win if we don't have you on our side," Sunathri said.

Garrick did not reply.

After several moments, she sighed and, like Darien before her, walked back to camp, her boots whipping through the grass.

It rained the next morning.

The camp woke up wet, and went about their well-practiced ritual of loading supplies and preparing their animals. The dampness around them muted all sound.

Garrick sat beside the creek and ate stale bread.

Sunathri came to him. She said nothing. Merely sat silently beside him until he finished eating.

"It's no use," he finally said. "I'm going on my own."

"We'll leave you a horse," she replied.

"I don't want one."

"You'll need to move quickly."

"I intend to go back to Caledena and gather back the one I left behind."

Sunathri's silence grew awkward once again.

"Don't you have to go?" he asked.

"I'm not leaving until you do."

Garrick gave a soft chuckle. "You'll make me be the one to walk away, will you?"

"Does that threaten you?"

"No," Garrick said. But inside he felt pressure. A band of fifty people would not move until he left them behind. *Actions and consequences.*

"The Torean House needs to be together if it is to survive," Sunathri said in a soft tone. "And together it needs to stand for something. What we stand for, Garrick, is the freedom of each person to find who they are for themselves. You may not believe this, but look around us. Nothing holds these people here but that thought. You can leave us, but we will never leave you, nor will we fight you unless you take an active side against us."

"I understand."

Garrick stood and helped her up.

"Where will you go?" he asked.

"The less you know of us, the less danger we can put you in."

"And the less danger I can put you in," he replied.

"That, too," she said.

He nodded. "Good luck."

"Luck to you, also."

Sunathri's eyes blazed with fierce pride.

In the distance, Darien stood with the Torean wizards, his arms crossed, and his father's sword sheathed along one leg.

Garrick turned away and walked into the forest heading northward, walking alone, back toward the city where he had a promise to keep.

When Darien asked Garrick if he was going to become a vigilante, the question irked him.

The word itself—vigilante—seemed sharp and ugly. It held a sense of danger, a hazy aura of radicalism that didn't appeal to him. The concept of vigilantism felt unyielding and rash. Vigilantes were angry people. Unpredictable men. Not swayed by fact. Vigilantes, by definition, were not rational.

But despite such prejudices, by the time he returned to Caledena, Garrick had decided Elman would die.

What unnerved him most was how at peace he had become with the idea. He had never made such a cold-blooded decision before, but Elman had killed Alistair, and he would have killed Garrick and Darien if it weren't for the Freeborn rescuers. Call it justice, call it self-defense, or call it a natural consequence of action, it didn't matter to Garrick. The orders weren't going to let him simply fade into the woods to live the solitary life he wanted to live, and since he didn't plan to be tied to a group, he couldn't see a different way out. So he would become a vigilante for as long as he needed to be one—

which he assumed would be until the orders stopped chasing Toreans.

And Elman would be his first target.

Yes, Elman had to die.

So Garrick walked through patches of thicket, dense woods, and overgrown trails with nothing but the calls of birds and the scurrying of rodents as his partners. He got a late start, so the nighttime sky was crystalline and dark by the time he arrived again at Caledena's gates. The song of cicadas filled the air, and dim moonlight made the city more shadow than passage. His skin tingled in the chill despite —or maybe because of—his body's adjustments to keep him warm.

He cast magic that silenced his footsteps, and he slipped through the woods at the edge of the city, pressing against walls of dry wood and gliding through alleys and across rutted streets as silently as a cat.

The city smelled of refuse. It felt like a cancer.

A derelict slept fitfully at the mouth of a nearby alleyway. Garrick's life force wanted to reach out to the man, but he was not there for charity. He pushed himself to focus on Elman and his Lectodinian siblings. With the mage's headquarters in shambles, Hersha Padiglio's old mansion was the most likely place for Elman to be.

A few minutes later, Garrick stood in the shadows of an alley just outside the manor. Lights blazed from the building. Three sentries standing inside the surrounding fence confirmed his assumption that Elman had moved in.

There would be more sentries, of course. And mages.

A horse whinnied nearby, and the earthy scent of manure brought a grin to Garrick's face. The stable was occupied.

He set a mage gate and let his dark energy free. One sentry was hungry, another was thinking about a woman he had seen earlier in the day. Garrick held the guards' life forces in his mind as if they were clay. One thought, and he could kill these men. One thought, and he could step unimpeded into the Lectodinian's headquarters.

He had killed before.

The idea did not bother him now.

What did that say about him?

As he closed his mind to that question, a sharp cry came from inside the stable, followed by a thump like a sack of flour hitting the ground.

The guards came to immediate alert.

Garrick slipped into deeper shadows to watch as two of them went into the stables, and emerged wrestling with a small form between them.

"What is it, Peitar?" the third guard asked.

"Just a punk," came the reply. "Stop kicking, boy. You're making it worse on yourself."

The sound of a backhanded slap cracked against the night.

"Nooooo," the boy whined.

It was Will, the stable boy who had kept Kalomar.

Will's youthful essence overwhelmed Garrick's senses. The heat that welled across the boy's cheek tasted bitter. He felt shame in that heat, he felt weakness.

The men laughed.

"Teach him a lesson, Peitar."

Another slap came, then another.

Garrick moved without conscious thought, casting a net of magic that flowed over Peitar. As he strode toward the group, he spoke more magic. The guard farthest from him swung his sword and caught Garrick high on the shoulder, but Garrick funneled the guard's life force into his arm and the gash immediately closed.

Peitar dropped the boy and reached for his sword.

"Alert!" he called. "Alert!"

Garrick cut the guard down with a blast of pure energy, causing the other guards to retreat into the manor.

He grabbed the boy by the shoulder and lifted him to his feet.

Will flinched but did not run.

A clamor came from inside. Voices called to each other. His surprise was gone. The guards would soon be accompanied by mages, and, while Garrick felt prepared for them he did not care to create such a stir if Will were in the middle of it.

Stand and fight, or ensure he could save the boy?

He was here to deal with Elman.

Here to exact his revenge.

But now a crimson welt glowed across Will's cheek, and Garrick felt chaos building in the city around him. Elman could wait.

"Let's get out of here," he said. "Where's Kalomar?"

"Follow me, sir," Will said as he set his jaw and raced to the stables.

Kalomar whinnied as they opened the stall.

"Can you ride bareback, sir?" the boy asked.

Garrick leapt atop Kalomar and gave Will a hand up. "I can manage," he said, smiling despite the moment. He dug heels into the horse's flanks. The boy's life force nearly burned him as it pressed into his chest. "Duck down!" Garrick called out as they bolted from the stables.

Will did as he was told.

"Go, boy!" Will yelled to the horse.

Mages and swordsmen poured from the manor building. Kalomar's hooves beat upon the dirt road. Blasts of magical fire sizzled around them as they charged through the streets. Will leaned into the animal's motion, and Garrick shifted around to protect the boy as well as he could.

A shimmering blue barrier blocked their path ahead.

Garrick pulled at his link and cast an electric burst of life force that destroyed the barrier.

Kalomar ran harder.

"To the hills," Garrick said, pointing.

Will buried his head along Kalomar's neck and turned the animal. They charged through Caledena, out into the open, then disappeared into the wood. A few moments later, when Garrick could see no one following, he slowed the horse to protect him from stumbling in the darkness.

"You did it!" Will squealed. "We escaped!"

"Don't celebrate too quickly, boy," Garrick said. "The orders will not be happy about being on the short end again."

Will tried to give a solemn nod, but Garrick saw his face was still bright with victory.

"Come on," Garrick said, prodding Kalomar. "We need to put more distance between us before morning comes."

SEVEN

Kalomar walked with a steady rhythm. His black mane shifted with his stride.

Garrick pulled Will against him to keep the boy warm. They turned east after a short distance, then turned south some distance later. Garrick considered casting a spell to hide their progress, but any casting was just as likely to draw attention as to ward them against it. He was more worried about avoiding Elman's magic than anything else.

"I knew you would come back, Master Garrick."

"How?"

"You promised me," Will replied.

Garrick laughed. The boy had an honesty about him that was easy to admire.

"I think we're going to be fine," he said.

"I heard them talking about you, sir."

"Oh? And what did they say?"

"They said there's a bounty on you."

"With any luck, it will be more than ten coppers by now."

"What do you mean?"

Garrick glanced at the boy. Will reminded him of when he was a stable boy. "Don't worry about it," he said. "There are things worse than having a price on your head."

"Name one."

Being invisible, he thought.

"Getting slapped around by a guard," he finally replied.

"Oh, that's nothing."

"No, it's not," Garrick replied. "And don't let anybody tell you differently."

Kalomar's ear twitched.

Garrick pulled up short and gave a curse.

He felt mages scattered about, fifteen—or maybe twenty. They surrounded them, hidden in the dark gullies or behind copses of trees. He could feel them all, but he could only get his bearings on maybe half at once before they started to slip away.

"Wh—" Will's cry was cut short, and his body went rigid against Garrick's chest.

The blue light of Lectodinian magic glowed around them.

Garrick was free to move, but Will was frozen solid before him.

"We're going to do this a little differently this time," the familiar voice of a familiar mage came as he stepped into view. Several others followed in his wake.

"Elman," Garrick said. "I've missed you."

The Lectodinian walked with a noticeable limp, his gaze poisonous, his face freshly scarred.

"You're hurt," Garrick said with deadpan clarity and as much false concern as he could muster.

"Yes," Elman said, his finger tracing a long scar that ran down his cheekbone. "The creature you brought into the city killed ten mages before we could bring it down."

"I'll be more careful next time."

Elman smirked. "As you have no doubt already determined, Garrick, I have many mages scattered about, each with magic targeted directly at the boy. One mistake from you, and he will die."

Garrick set his gates and felt the Lectodinian mages. He could handle most of them quickly, but there were too many, and—as Elman suggested—they would surely get to Will before he could take them all down.

"What do you want, Elman?"

"I'm taking you back to Caledena."

"You plan to execute me?"

"Are you always this dramatic, Garrick?"

Garrick did not reply.

Elman sighed. "Personally, I think that would be the wiser path to take. But Lord Esta feels a need to speak to you directly. I hope you are adequately honored."

"Who is Lord Esta?"

"Tsk-tsk, Garrick. Even the poorest of mages should know the name of the Lord Superior of the Lectodinian order."

Garrick stared at Elman.

If the Lectodinian superior wanted to talk with him, he had more than a bit of bargaining room.

Elman continued.

"The boy stays where he is, but you can get off the horse."

Garrick nodded. "Be good," he whispered to Will as he slid off Kalomar's back. "And don't worry."

Four mages walked cautiously forward, each concentrating on the spell work that held Will frozen. One looped a rope around Kalomar's neck. With a firm hand, he turned the horse around.

A command from Elman sent them back toward Caledena.

GARRICK WAS unrestrained as Elman led the mages and guardsmen through the woods south of Caledena. The lack of binding was a message itself.

I own you, it said. *I can control you without even touching you.*

The forest was still dark and the trees obliterated much of the sky, but what little he could see was littered with stars. Lectodinian boots whipped through the dew-wet grass with a ripping sound. It was a frustrating feeling to have the freedom to move but to know he was truly powerless to stop the Lectodinian mage from killing the boy if that was what Elman desired to do.

Kalomar plodded along.

Will stayed seated, staring straight ahead.

It didn't take a historian to guess why Zutrian Esta wanted to speak with him. Garrick was god-touched. Esta would offer him the chance to join the Lectodinian order.

It was good to be wanted, he thought with no little sarcasm.

A gnat flew in his face, and he tried to blow it away. It persisted, though, flying into his ear with an annoying vibration.

"You're turning into more trouble than you're worth," the gnat said. "Perhaps I should just let the Lectodinians destroy you."

Garrick's eyes widened.

Braxidane!

"He will do it, you know?" the gnat buzzed. "Zutrian?"

Do what?

"Kill you."

Garrick thought nothing for several for several moments. Then, *are you always this dramatic?*

"Where have I heard that before?"

Garrick couldn't keep a grimace from his face, but neither Elman nor the other Lectodinians made any reaction.

"He won't allow a true Torean to leave his sight alive, and I know better than to think you will agree to work with the Lectodinians."

I'm tired of this, Braxidane. If you're here to help me, get to it. Otherwise, get out of my ear.

"You're no child anymore. I can't help you every time you get yourself into trouble."

Then leave me alone.

"As you wish."

The gnat flew off, and Garrick regretted his anger immediately. *Braxidane! Braxidane! Come back here.*

He received no answer, though, and felt desperately stupid.

An idea came then.

Braxidane's transition to animal form was a true changing of the material that made up his body. How else could the planewalker enter his ear? And that transformation had allowed him to slip unnoticed through Elman's defenses. Garrick didn't think he could manage the transformation process, but perhaps he could create a distraction that would do the job—an illusion that would work just as well.

He channeled life force through his gates. Then he touched his link to the plane of magic and poured magestuff into that stream.

It was like pairing water and oil, but he kept them under control while maintaining the smoothness of his movement. With focus, the two magics knit into a silky-smooth essence, and the faint aroma of honey grew.

He was ready.

He started with his feet and worked his way upward.

When he was finished, Garrick took a moment to gather himself. Then he stepped aside.

Kalomar nickered, but none of the mages made any move.

He glanced at his illusion.

Seeing himself almost caused him to break the moment.

His face was so angular. His lanky body had filled in and been toughened by the road and by the battlefield. The muscles of his arms were corded and etched with a wiry strength.

Was that really him?

He looked old. Like a man.

It was truly strange.

The illusion held, though. None of Elman's mages reacted when he stepped aside, and it continued to walk with the same fluid motion that was Garrick's gait.

Striding beside the congregation, Garrick spread his spellwork over Will and Kalomar. The horse's ears twitched, but the beast remained silent. Once Garrick was certain the entire illusion would hold, he turned Kalomar toward the deep forest.

The movement transferred the mage's hold from Will to his doppelganger, and the boy's eyes grew wide.

Garrick pressed a finger to his lips.

Will showed his understanding.

Garrick led Kalomar away, taking pains to avoid any accidental brush against the attendants. When they were free from the pack and a safe distance into the woods, Garrick brought Kalomar to a halt and let the boy down.

The Lectodinians continued onward through the wood.

The morning grew still in the small clearing. A stream gurgled nearby, and the rhythmic cadence of insects calling rose throughout the wood.

Garrick finally let out a sigh of relief.

"All right, Braxidane," he said aloud. "We need to talk."

EIGHT

A pinpoint of golden light appeared in the middle of the clearing. It expanded, becoming a gleaming globe, then dissolved to reveal Braxidane's willowy form—a young man, this time, wearing a green tunic, leggings, and a thin rapier that hung from his belt.

Will clung to Garrick's side like a frightened cub.

Garrick put his arm around the boy's shoulder.

"That was nice work," Braxidane said. "You are learning well. Someday you'll come to trust that your magic is bound by only your imagination."

"What price do you pay for intervening here?"

Braxidane chuckled. "You truly *are* learning, aren't you—or did you just guess that?"

"I believe you are the one who taught me there are *only* actions and consequences."

"Well," Braxidane huffed. "Apparently you have a brilliant teacher."

"So, I ask again, what consequence do you suffer for your action of interfering with me?"

"You are the consequence, Garrick."

"What does that mean?"

"I didn't start this chain of events, but I would be a poor example of a god if I didn't take advantage of such an opportunity."

"You are no god," Garrick responded, quoting his teachings from Alistair. "You are nothing but a creature who can move between the many planes of existence.

"But," Braxidane ignored Garric, and spoke on, "you are correct in one way, you see. *Gods* cannot easily intervene in the activities of individual planes. But sometimes one of us desires some specific power, or sometimes just grows interested to the point they are willing to pay the price to enter a plane. And when that happens, he—or she—opens the gate for others to follow."

"Don't be so convoluted," Garrick said.

"I apologize. I forget your need for simplicity."

"You're saying," Garrick replied, "that when a planewalker crosses into a plane, others can follow."

Braxidane's expression was a look of ebullience. "There is hope for you, yet, Garrick. One god opening a path makes it easier for others to follow—the need for balance in all things is a natural one, you see? Actions and consequences."

"Yes," Garrick said. "I see."

"You must work harder to understand this, Garrick. This need for balance permeates everything."

"Everything?"

"Indeed."

Braxidane hesitated then, waiting. His expression was sharp and questioning as if wanting to see what Garrick might say.

A truth built within him.

"The orders obtained their god-touched mages first."

"Yes, Garrick, there is *indeed* hope for you. If others of my ilk hadn't provided the orders with their mages first, I would not have been inclined to give this power to you. You are the balance, you see. You are the consequence."

"Lucky me."

"Yes, lucky you."

"Why me? Surely there were better options."

"You made yourself available."

Garrick grimaced. "I'm not naive enough to think you would choose an apprentice based on mere convenience."

"Do not sell yourself short, Garrick. I'm pleased. You are so much bolder today than the mere lad who cried out for help a few months ago was."

"That's no answer."

"I feel no need to answer such a senseless question."

"A magewar is brewing, Braxidane. There are no senseless questions." Garrick stopped then. A sudden chill ran up his back. "You're all just playing with us, aren't you? The planewalkers. A war between us wouldn't bother you at all. You're all just dallying."

Braxidane smiled.

"The other god-touched mages came from other planewalkers. And it was those planewalkers stepping into Adruin that *permitted you* to follow." Garrick's dander was up now. His mind was following the breadcrumbs Braxidane had left behind. "But when you add it all up, you're all just playing a game."

Braxidane shrugged. "We play only those games that the people of the planes play themselves. My brothers and sisters are the ones fostering the mage hunt. I'm helping you. But none of these things seem foreign to your people. It's all happened before, after all."

Garrick paused, letting this idea sink in. Thoughts jumbled as he looked at the planewalker but he could not form a proper question. "It all seems so senseless."

"You want senseless, Garrick? I'll tell you what senseless is. Senseless is the Freeborn being obliterated by the orders' champions without your help—*that* is what senseless is."

"You want me to join them?"

"It seems prudent."

"What will happen if I don't?"

"Your friends will die."

"Why should *you* care?"

"The question, Garrick, is: Why do *you* care? And the question is: How long can you persist in thinking you don't matter?"

Anger spiked in him then.

Garrick was nobody. He had always been nobody. He was barely out of apprenticehood. A neophyte. Yet, now he was actually capable of changing things, and, for the first time, his gut was telling him he could make a difference in the world. But how much of this feeling true? And how much was actually his? Braxidane owned him, after all. This conversation alone told him that much. How much of this thinking was his own?

Braxidane expected things.

Darien, too.

And Sunathri. And the men and women of the entire Freeborn camp.

Garrick thought of Darien's inner strength. He recalled the purity of conviction in Suni's gaze as she pressed him to join her cause—a cause she had created wholly from within herself. He remembered the force of Will's youthful life.

They were all so full of hope. All so certain of things.

He wished he could be that way.

They did need him, though. He felt their need, and their expectation as if they were the dead weight of stones on his chest.

Their hope was false, though. Their expectation was wasted. He had no idea how to help beat back the orders' aggression.

And Braxidane was right about another thing, too—if the other god-touched mages were anything as powerful as he was, they could be devastating in battle. No opposing force could stand against that kind of power in the hands of a mage of real status and real experience. If the orders were planning to take the whole of Adruin, the Freeborn would be destroyed.

"I can't join the Freeborn," Garrick said. "But I'll do what I can."

"That sounds like a start."

Garrick set a defiant jaw. "I'll take life only under just conditions, though."

Braxidane's grin spread over his lips slowly. "It will go better for you if you remember there is no such thing as a just condition."

"Yes, there is," Garrick said. "Justice is the natural consequence of abusing power."

Braxidane opened his arms to the nighttime and gave a wide smile. "Who am I to argue with such logic?"

Garrick glared. "I'm not doing this to give you comfort in your logic."

"I don't care about your motives, Garrick. But since you have decided to help, you should know that the Freeborn are in Dorfort as we speak."

Garrick nodded, glancing south toward the city.

When he returned his gaze to the planewalker, Braxidane had blinked out of existence.

BRAXIDANE'S DISAPPEARANCE left both Garrick and Will in stunned silence.

Garrick looked at the boy and tousled his hair.

"Hey!" Will called, putting his hand to his head. "Who was that, Master Garrick?"

"I'll tell you about him later," Garrick said. "The Lectodinians will see through that illusion soon enough, so right now we had best get on the move."

"Yes, sir."

He grabbed the rope around Kalomar's neck and stroked the horse's flank.

"But, Will."

"Yes, sir?"

"Just call me Garrick. All right? No 'sir' and no 'master.' Just Garrick."

"Whatever you say, sir."

Garrick glared at the boy, and Will giggled.

"Sorry, Master Garrick." He giggled again.

Garrick couldn't help but smile. It felt good to be with the boy. They mounted up, Garrick first, then Will.

"So, are we going to Dorfort?" Will asked, his smile growing wide and toothy.

"Yes. It will be good to see the city again. I have some unfinished business there."

"I've never been to Dorfort. Will it be very exciting?"

"Yes," Garrick said as the boy settled back into his chest. "I'm sure it will all be very exciting."

NINE

"I don't know what happened, Lord Superior," Elman said with fear in his voice. "I've had my hands on Garrick twice now, and twice he has slipped away."

The mirror before him showed Zutrian Esta. The superior's eyes were sharp points and his lips were wrinkled up into webs of age. The lord superior's gaze alone might burn holes into him.

"Tell me exactly what happened *this* time," Zutrian Esta said.

Elman recounted the evening's efforts. He described how he had captured Garrick, and brought him back to Caledena to make him available for the discussion that he and the lord superior were having right now, then having the mage, the boy, and the horse all disappear into thin air upon reaching the city.

Elman finished the story, his palms up, his voice nasal and whining. "He *is* god-touched, after all," Elman said. "His magic is different from others."

Another unhappy expression crossed Zutrian's face.

Elman continued.

"I've been studying Garrick for some time now, though, Lord Esta," he said, pausing to lick his lips. "As you might expect, this has become quite personal for me. I've had spies working his case, and I think I know where he will go. I would like authorization to hunt him down one more time."

"Where will Garrick head?"

Elman's eyes glittered in the candlelight.

"To Dorfort, Lord Esta. He has lived much of his life in that area. He will go to a young woman's house."

"A woman?"

"Her name is Arianna. The daughter of a farmer and blacksmith. Garrick had a relationship with her before this all began."

Zutrian nodded slowly, information settling. He raised a bushy eyebrow.

"You have approval to follow your plan. But we cannot continue to fall on our faces before the Koradictines, Elman. Any error this time will result in severe punishment."

"I understand, Lord Superior. I will not fail."

CHAPTER

TEN

The sun was setting as Garrick and Will entered Dorfort, the city known as the crown jewel of eastern Adruin. It was a sprawling metropolis that grew along the Blue Lake, its architecture a mixture of brick, stone, thatch, and wood, an eclectic collection of architectures that stretched to the sky and hugged the coast. Smoke from forges, tanneries, bakeries, and restaurants rose through air that was heavy with scents of harbor brine and the spices that were being unloaded from trading ships that were newly docked.

Will squirmed in the saddle. He was not used to such long hours on a horse.

"Are we going to see Lord Ellesadil?" Will asked.

"It's too late, today," Garrick replied. "Tonight we'll settle into the city. Perhaps we can see the lord tomorrow."

"Will we find your friends?"

"You mean the Freeborn?"

"Yeah, the Freeborn."

The boy had asked incessantly about Darien and the Freeborn while they traveled. His eyes had gone wide as Garrick told of their adventures in Arderveer and how the Torean House had rescued them in Caledena. To Will, the Freeborn were swashbuckling pirates, bigger than life.

"I don't think we'll have to find them so much as *they* will find us."

"That doesn't make sense."

"It will," Garrick replied. "Until then, you're just going to have to trust me."

The answer didn't satisfy the boy, but he was used to being told what to do, so he let it pass.

Garrick was happy for the moment of silence. Will was a young lad with a thousand questions about a thousand topics, and he had asked them all during their trip south. Though his questions made their travels annoying at times, Garrick saw the better parts of himself in Will—this boy with his blondish hair and the freckles on his cheeks. Will was old enough to fend for himself, but young enough that Garrick felt pain at the idea of him being alone.

Will was a problem, though.

Garrick wanted to keep the boy safe, but that would be difficult when he could barely stay out of trouble himself. It was unwise to have a young boy involved in his life now, too, but he didn't know what else to do. Will reminded him of the other apprentices under Alistair. He couldn't imagine leaving him behind.

He thought of this during the all-too-few quiet moments of their travels but never came to any answers.

Eventually, they came to a business district and a tavern called the Golden Gourd.

Laughter came from its open windows.

"We'll need a room for the night," Garrick said as he slid off of Kalomar. "Wait here."

He slipped the proprietor a silver, then he returned to find Will staring with hungry eyes at the tavern section of the building. The smell of freshly baked bread and cooking meat wafted from inside. Voices rolled from an open window.

He helped Will off the horse.

"Get Kalomar comfortable in the stable, and meet me inside for dinner," Garrick said.

"I'll be right there," Will said.

The boy took off to take care of his chores, leaving Garrick to enter the tavern alone.

ELEVEN

Garrick took a table at the back corner of the inn and sat so he could view most of the room. He waved the barmaid to bring food. The room was warm with the heat of patrons who came and went in a steady flow. It was loud with voices. The smell of exotic tobaccos and roasted meats gave it a comforting veil.

He was not physically drained, but he was tired of thinking.

It was good to relax.

His mind wandered. Fingers of his life force writhed within him, still active, still keeping the darkness of his hunger at bay. But it *was* fading. Slowly. It was like a timing glass inside him with its sand slipping silently into the darkness.

He looked out the tavern's west-facing window and saw the setting sun had streaked the high clouds with rays of orange and lavender. It was about this time of day when it all started. He remembered it well, that evening with Arianna. Springtime had just begun to burst across the land.

Arianna.

Was she working at the Ladle this evening? He wanted to see her, but knew that would be a disaster.

"I'm back!" Will yelled.

Garrick's heart leapt into his throat.

"Don't do that!" he snapped at the boy.

Will's face dropped. "I'm sorry, Master Garrick, sir."

Garrick calmed himself. "It's all right, Will. You were just having fun. I shouldn't have yelled at you, but you caught me off guard, and you need to understand that there are times when I can … cause problems … when I get surprised."

Will's cheeks grew red.

"I'm sorry," He said.

"Don't worry about it."

Garrick smiled and tousled Will's hair. The boy complained about it, but Garrick saw he enjoyed it, too, so he did it as often as he could.

"But, please, will you drop the *master* and the *sir?*"

"Yes, sir … er, Garrick," Will said, giggling again.

The barmaid brought sausage stew, boiled greens, and a loaf of bread.

Both Garrick and Will used the grainy bread to sop up what remained of the stew. When they were finished, Will's face shone with new color.

"Garrick, sir?"

Garrick glared. "Yes?"

"I mean, Garrick." Will's grin was sheepish. "Can you teach me magic?"

Garrick reacted sharply. The boy didn't know what he was asking. There was no way he was taking on an apprentice now. He glanced around the room. The tavern was filled, but no one seemed to have heard Will's question.

"That is a conversation we can have someplace more private."

"News!" a voice bellowed from the center of the room.

The speaker stood in the open center of the room, wearing a tunic of sun-faded cloth with sleeves that were ragged at the shoulders. His breeches were stained with grease. His hair was dark, his eyes so brown they disappeared into the shadows of his pupils. His browned skin, leathered by the sun, marked him as a sailor.

The room hushed.

"There is war in the west," he announced.

Voices buzzed.

"They say Captain Parathay, a Lectodinian magis slinger, has taken Whitestone and Warville! He's got an army of hired blades and hundreds of his order at his command, and if progress has continued as they were, by now he's deep into the Wizardpeaks."

"How do you know this?" a farmer asked.

"Seen the army with my own eyes, I did. I come fresh from Whitestone on a run of the freight galley *Regent*."

The storyteller bent at the waist and peered into the crowd.

"The warriors in that city are hardened men. If'n you get in their way they're likely to cut your throat as they are to hear you out. No man or woman in Whitestone leaves their cabin by moonlight now without being hunted for sport."

"Ghastly," a woman said.

The storyteller poked his finger in her direction. "'Deed it is, ma'am. 'Deed it is. But it gets worse than that."

"Tell on!"

"I've not seen this with my own eyes, so I can't vouch for it personally. But I hear tell stories that a *Koradictine* mage named Jormar el'Mor has another army collected in the northwest, and is running through the Badwall Canyons."

"A Koradictine?" a man called.

"Magewar?" the woman said.

"'Swhat it sounds like to me. 'Swhat it sounds like, indeed."

A deep voice interrupted the ensuing clamor. "No magewar's brewing today, least not between the orders." The voice belonged to a huge man with a bald head and a bristly beard who was sitting at a table along the far side of the room. He was dressed for the hills. A half-eaten slab of meat and a mug of ale sat before him. His sword lay across the table to his left.

"Why say you that, sir?" the storyteller said.

The ranger drank from his mug before speaking. "Because the orders are working together."

The room was quiet for an instant, then the storyteller chuckled. "That's a fair joke, my friend."

The bald man shook his head. "It's no joke. Take a ride up Caledena way if you think I'm spinning tales. The viceroy is deposed and you'll find rune-marks of both orders scattered about town."

The original storyteller shook his head. "Strange happenings, if that's true."

The bald ranger replied, "No stranger than talk of the mad Torean the orders are searching for."

The air seemed to leave the room, and Garrick's heart rose to his throat. He glanced at Will, then the storyteller, then back to the bald man.

The storyteller bowed to the bald man. "Perhaps, fine sir, *you'd* like to take the floor? I, for one, am more intrigued by your story than by mine."

The ranger turned so his back was against the wall. He picked his teeth with a fingernail. "They could be the same story, my friend. Mine's not complete, so I'm not sure what to make of it. But I was in Caledena when the Lectodinians and Koradictines took the city. And I was there two days ago when their place was torn apart by Toreans —a new banner, as I understand it, and a new banner the orders don't much like. But mostly I hear that the Torean banner raided the city to retrieve a pair of mages from the viceroy, and I hear one of those mages has magic that rips souls straight from the bodies of them that own 'em."

"Sjesko!" The woman up front gasped.

"And that boy out west," said another.

"Could that Torean be the same demon?" the first woman asked.

"I don't know those stories," the bald man replied. "So I couldn't say, but if the mage that done those was a lanky young man with wild hair, there's reasonable chance they're one and the same."

Garrick shriveled inside.

He pressed himself back into the corner and hunched his shoulders.

"I understand the mage returned to Caledena last night, stole back his horse, and kidnapped a stable boy. And that he killed fifteen men doing it."

Will's expression grew animated as understanding dawned on his face.

Garrick gave him a tight-lipped shake of his head.

He glanced around the room. Fifteen dead mages was farcical. That news was probably Elman's doing, information distributed to stir up the locals.

"It's him," a young female voice said.

It was the woman who served their food, standing in the kitchen doorway, her crooked finger pointing at Garrick.

Heads whirled to face him.

He was in shadow, but that wasn't enough to hide him.

A month ago, perhaps even a day ago, he would have wilted or maybe played dumb by ignoring the accusation and hoping it would die away. Maybe a week ago he would have cast a spell and run. But Garrick felt something different now. He wanted people to know the truth. This was who he was now. He wanted to make things right. These people did not deserve to be toyed with. They deserved to know what was happening, and at that moment Garrick felt he was finally in the very place he was meant to be.

He stepped from the shadows so that any in the tavern could see him.

The crowd gasped.

Stools screeched against the floor, and voices fell silent.

"You are right, sir," Garrick said striding to the middle of the room. His tall form and his wiry body gave him an aura of intensity. These people would listen to what he had to say. "The orders have bonded together, and they are hunting Toreans. I wish I could say things were going well for our independent house, but I can't. I can, however, forewarn you that when the orders finish with the Torean House, there *will* be magewar like none you have ever seen, and if it is not stopped now it *will* change the plane forever."

"Demon!" the woman said. "You killed the boy!"

"It was an accident," Garrick said. "Purely an accident."

"Devil!" her husband joined, standing protectively in front of his wife and holding a talisman before him.

The room erupted.

Life force stirred within the chaos. Garrick pushed it back, though, and raised his arms as if to cast a spell.

"Stop it!" he yelled, his voice deep and powerful. "Just stop it."

The room settled into an edgy and uncomfortable quiet. Fear crossed every face around the room.

"I am no demon. If I were, I would have already supped on your souls. I am merely a man, though. I wish no one harm."

"What of the dead in Caledena?" the ranger asked.

Garrick turned to the bald man.

"If you're going to tell stories about me, I suggest you get them right. Only a few men died in my raid last night, and those few died only because they gave violence to the boy who now travels with me. And before you feel for them, you might consider the thousands of people the orders slaughtered in Arderveer a fortnight prior."

The room was now quiet except for the crackling fire pit and city noises that drifted in through the open windows.

"Come here, Will."

The boy complied, and Garrick put his arm around Will's shoulder.

"The boy and I are going to leave, quietly and peacefully. Make of that what you will. But heed my warnings. It is important that you listen to the news this man brings, and it is important, too, that you make your minds for yourself. Koradictine and Lectodinian rule will be upon you before you know it, and it will be only through people like the Torean mages of the Freeborn, or maybe through independent people like me and like you, that Adruin as you know it may be saved."

The crowd moved away as Garrick led Will to the doorway.

"Be careful, wizard," the bald man said from afar. "News of this speech will travel."

"Thank you," Garrick said.

Then he took Will by the shoulder and guided him out of the tavern.

The nighttime air was cool, and the streets still busy.

"The orders will know where we are in the time it takes a man to run across town," Garrick said as he led Will to the stables. "So we had best get on the move."

"Are you a demon?" Will asked.

"No, Will," Garrick replied. "But sometimes it feels that way."

"Are you afraid?"

He looked at the boy and felt a noose tightening around his neck. Until recently he thought that noose was looped only around his own neck, but he felt differently now. Listening to the story and seeing it resonate through the room gave him a small glimpse of what this meant to the world he knew. If planewalkers were involved, that meant this was a big noose, a noose that was looped around the necks of every person on the plane. That included the necks of every Lectodinian and Koradictine mage on the plane, too, though they may not know it.

Alistair, with his penchant for isolation, would have bristled at this news that kept falling around him like pieces of a single puzzle. "There's always a bigger demon," Alistair would have muttered as he tweaked up a warding spell.

Garrick thought about planewalkers, about Arderveer, and about Elman waiting for him in Caledena. He thought about his god-touched magic, and he wondered where Darien and Sunathri might be. The orders were coming for him, and if he stayed with the Free-born he was putting his friends at risk. On the other hand, as long as Garrick was alive the orders had a common enemy and would focus less on the Freeborn. Perhaps he was, therefore, the last barrier to full-scale war.

It was a strange thing to be both a target and a security blanket, but that was what he was.

"Yes," Garrick replied finally to Will. "I'm afraid of a lot of things."

"That didn't go as I had hoped," Garrick said to Will as they rode on through the city.

The night was growing dark.

"What are we going to do now?" Will said.

"It's too dangerous at the Inn," Garrick replied. "So we'll find a place out here to pass the night."

"Out here?"

Will's expression of fear told Garrick all he needed to know about the boy's opinion of sleeping in the alleyway of a big city.

"I'll watch over you. You'll be fine, I promise."

"And we'll see Darien tomorrow?"

"Maybe."

The questions were beginning to annoy him again. "We'll go to the university," he said. "And if Darien wants to join us, he'll find us there."

"The university? What are we going to do at the university?"

"We're going to try to learn as much as we can about the orders, Will. Where they came from, who they are, and where they might be today. Consider it your first lesson in magic, all right? Does that sound fun?"

"Yeah!"

Garrick was happy Will couldn't see his expression from his seat in front of him. He wasn't going to tell Will that he needed to learn more about the orders because he had decided to go mage hunting.

And he wasn't going to tell Will that he was going to find the boy a new place to live, that Garrick was going to leave Will there while he went off on that hunt. There are things that boys of a dozen or so years don't understand, and Garrick wasn't ready to face any of those things tonight.

"But for now we're going to find you a place to sleep."

Garrick knew this city well and figured they would be safest in an alleyway, or maybe against a shore dock. He selected an alley and propped a discarded crate against a brick wall to give Will a place to sleep. Kalomar stood at the end of the alleyway, hitched loosely to a post.

With his life force draining, Garrick did not sleep. But as he huddled against the wall using discarded fabric as a blanket, he slipped along the edge of lucidity. Dreams played at the edge of his senses.

Darien swept his blood-bathed sword toward the neck of a burly creature.

The thing's head tumbled to the ground, and as it rolled forward its features grew more human and more similar to Darien's. When it came to a halt Garrick saw it was Thale, Darien's brother ...

Sunathri sat on a throne of polished stone. She twisted and pulled against restraints made of black and purple vines, but her efforts served only to draw the vines tighter. A snake slithered at her feet, twining slowly up one of the chair's legs. She couldn't speak, but her eyes were wide with terror. Garrick pulled a knife from his belt and sliced at the straps, freeing her just as the serpent buried its fangs deeply into her neck ...

As Sunathri screamed, another serpent wrapped around his leg, its mouth gaping open, fangs prepared to strike ...

Garrick screamed himself awake.

A man was there, squatted beside him and shaking him by the ankle.

Garrick scuttled away, preparing magic.

"Calm yourself, Garrick," the man said. "If I had designs to kill you, you would never have woken up."

The voice was deep and familiar. It was the bald ranger from the inn.

Garrick breathed easier. His back hurt where the rough brick had bitten into it. His muscles ached from sitting on hard ground.

"How do you know my name?"

"Stories about you are growing more numerous than you may be comfortable with," the man replied. "You'll need to be sharper about where you sleep in the future. An alley is too easy a target."

A dark body lay nearby.

Garrick nodded at it.

"Your work?"

The man grinned, his teeth white despite the shadows. "Lectodinian by the look of the brand."

"Thank you," Garrick said.

"I've never been too fond of the orders."

"I'm glad of that."

The bald man took a crab step over to the body, then reached around its waist to remove a belt and a sturdy dagger. He handed them to Garrick. "You'll need something other than your magic to protect you."

The blade was short and stubby—a weapon balanced for throwing. He slipped it into his belt loop.

"What do you want for your services?"

"Nothing."

Garrick gave him a quizzical glance.

"I figure you're on the right side, Garrick. At least you talk a good game, eh?"

"Thank you. I hope I can repay it someday."

The bald man glanced to the end of the alley. "You best be moving on," he said. Then the man was gone.

Will was irritable when Garrick roused him, but he got moving quickly at the idea of a dead body a few feet away.

"Where are we going?" Will asked as Garrick lifted the boy to Kalomar's back.

"We'll think of something."

He glanced to the east.

The morning was still a considerable time away.

They were probably safer if they got out of the city sprawl.

That's when he knew where he was going. It would be just for the evening, he told himself as he turned Kalomar to the west, and toward the sparse woodlands Garrick was so familiar with.

Arianna lived there—Arianna, her family, and her quiet life.

He thought about her and the one kiss they shared. He remembered the panic he felt as he cradled her bleeding head, the look of horror on her face when she saw what he'd done.

Arianna may never want to see him again, but he was drawn to her.

He wanted to see her one last time.

Will lolled in the saddle. His legs gave an involuntary dream jerk.

And, Garrick thought, still trying to justify his decision, even if Arianna wouldn't see him, perhaps Arianna's father would take the boy in. The man could always use another hand in the fields, or maybe Will would be better at dealing with the alchemy of the smithy shop.

Garrick smiled despite himself.

If nothing else, the woods should be a safe place for the boy to sleep tonight.

IT WASN'T UNTIL LATER, as they picked their way through the streets of Dorfort and into the dense trees, and as Will's head lolled back against his chest, that Garrick realized he had never even asked the man who had saved them for his name.

TWELVE

Elman grinned coldly as he watched Garrick and the boy ride through the woods. He was right! Garrick had come to the girl's home. The thought brought him more than joy. He *needed* to be right this time. To have been wrong would have been unthinkable.

He sat on his horse, waiting.

The air was cool and smelled of earth and damp wood. A half-moon hung high in the cloudless sky. The call of insects grew louder. It was a shame the boy had to be involved. But that was not his doing.

He cast a brief spell to send word to the others.

No prisoners.

As expected, Arianna's house was dark and draped in the shadow of trees. Hickory smoke wafted from the chimney, reminding him of simpler times when Arianna's family had accepted him as one of their own.

Garrick framed the boy with his arms and felt his head roll with the horse's motions.

"Are you all right, Garrick?" Will said in a sleepy voice.

"Yes. I'm fine," he said.

And he was.

Coming here had been the right thing to do. If he hadn't come here he would always wonder about her, always have doubts. But just seeing the place was enough. He didn't belong here anymore. He had changed, and it was time to turn the page. He would return tomorrow, though. He would return to see about leaving Will in such a proper place to grow up.

The idea made him happy.

As he finished the thought, a sharp crack rang out, and his life force became suddenly alert.

Will twisted in the saddle, peering into the darkness. "What—"

"Shh," Garrick hissed, setting his gates.

A dark form moved in the woods, dropping under cover before Garrick could identify it. He guided Kalomar away from the house and toward the forest.

His senses stretched out and he felt life force—humans. Lectodinians. First five, then ten, then twenty, and more, all mages, and all armed. Leaves rustled as the Lectodinians moved as one.

Garrick spoke and pulled at his link.

His magelight illuminated Elman's face.

The Lectodinian was casting, his lips moving, his hands cupped and crossed. Elman gave a sharp motion, and every mage in the clearing cast their sorcery at once.

Garrick funneled life force into a quick barrier that clashed with the barrage and sent a shower of sparks across the night. The Lectodinians poured more magic upon him, but Garrick's barrier was strong and they soon found themselves in a stalemate, a steady stream of Lectodinian sorcery flowing over the Torean's impervious shield.

"Hoping to make one more dash into your lover's arms?" Elman called.

Garrick ignored the taunt. "Hold tight," he said to Will as he spurred Kalomar.

The horse lowered his head and surged forward.

Garrick gritted his teeth and pushed his spell before him like a battering ram. A stream of Lectodinian flames flowed off the shield, searing the ground until Kalomar pulled to an abrupt halt.

Lectodinian magic still rained over his shield, but a gap emerged in their positions. Garrick angled for it, a path that took him toward Arianna's house.

A light came on inside.

No!

A bolt struck the tree next to them, and the trunk cracked before falling.

Kalomar screamed and leapt away to avoid being crushed.

The pounding of hooves thundered through Garrick's ears, and his heart pumped. He was losing ground. The Lectodinians had him running in circles. Their net was drawing tighter. His shield would not last forever.

The door to the house opened.

Arianna's father and brothers stepped onto the porch, each carrying curved blades.

"Go back inside!" Garrick yelled.

But her father bellowed something Garrick was unable to decipher, and did not retreat.

In the sudden lull, the mages cast a cloud of sorcerous blades that glinted around him like a nesthive of silver hornets.

He fortified his barricade, but the razors tore a hole in its fabric and more blue magic flared. Kalomar screamed in agony. Pain burned through Garrick's leg. He defended himself by sending a bolt of pure energy back in the direction the blast had come from, but there were so many of them—row upon row upon row of Lecto-dinian mages, and his life force was fading with each exertion.

He smelled the thick bile of his hunger stirring. Its essence was strong and firm, a dark beast rising through the depths of his night-mares, growing more powerful as time passed. It flexed its maw now, and its head swayed to and fro like a black dragon rising from the dead.

More magic flashed ahead of them.

Kalomar reared, throwing Garrick and Will into the air.

Garrick pulled Will around so he padded the boy's fall. His ankle made a sickening crunch as they landed, and the impact knocked the breath out of him.

"Run!" he yelled as best he could and pushed Will toward a bush.

Will scampered for cover.

The heat of his life force slid toward his injured ankle, but he didn't want to divert attention from the shield.

Another bolt of magic flared.

Kalomar screamed again, then fell heavily sideways.

Garrick tried to stand, but pain streaked his ankle.

His stomach churned, and the hunger inside him grew colder.

Hurried footsteps crashed through the brush—more mages. The Lectodinians had learned. They were taking no chances here—they had probably sent everything they could spare and then some.

It was over, though. He knew it was true.

He would lose here.

Garrick had just grown to believe he could take care of himself, and now he had been caught unprepared, yet again. No, that wasn't correct. He had been caught unprepared *because* he had begun to think he could handle himself.

It was the hunger that spoke to him loudest now—the dark, angry fury that lay just under his skin. He had to do something, and he had to do it now or he was going to lose everything.

Flames burst a few strides away.

He stood firmly despite the pain in his ankle. He funneled

magestuff from his link and pulled every bit of life force he could muster from inside. He spooled it all, waiting until he had enough energy built up, holding off, depleting himself until the darkness came forward in full measure.

He called on that hunger now, bringing it forward with a purpose. And, this time Garrick welcomed it. He dropped the shield around him, and he looked at the approaching mages through eyes on fire. He reached out with his wild magic, searching for every Lectodinian he could find, mapping the distance with that hunger, and feeling each target.

Arianna's father drew near, muttering curses and wielding his blade.

"Get away!" Garrick bellowed.

A Lectodinian blast struck Garrick in the chest, and he froze with pain as the blast seeped into his being. He gathered the spell's energy into himself, though, and Garrick poured it back into his spellwork. With a single thought, he unleashed a thunderclap—a raging torrent of silver-blue energy that snaked across the forest with a flickering strobe that froze everything in place.

One Lectodinian carried a predatory smile.

Another an expression of shock.

Garrick's spell took them all at once, the scintillating fingers of his magic snaking out and scoring them all full-force, the power of his sorcery fueled by anger and his need for vengeance. Energy sizzled. Life force mixed with sorcery to create a new breed of magic.

Screams echoed through the woods.

The trees bent in the wind.

Then it was over.

Garrick lay on the ground, gasping for breath, spent and unable to raise his head. It was dark, so dark. His cheek pressed hard against dirt and leaves. Hunger burned through his body. Braxidane's whisper was a bare breath that he couldn't decipher. Life force hung free over the woods, but he couldn't move and the hunger merely twisted inside his gut.

A footstep crunched a few feet away.

Elman's voice bled into Garrick's consciousness.

"That was an impressive display, Garrick. But now you will die."

The Lectodinian's tone said Elman had been hurt, but had somehow managed to fend off the brunt of Garrick's attack.

Elman spoke soft words of magic.

A sick green light flared about Garrick. His chest constricted. He tried to move, but could not. Faces from his past flashed into his mind.

I'm sorry, Garrick thought. He had done everything he could, defeated every Lectodinian but one, but it had not been enough.

Standing above him, Elman spoke the final syllables of his spell.

Blue flames burned in his palms.

A shadow of movement flashed at the edge of Garrick's vision.

Will!

The boy leapt from the brush, pulled the dagger from Garrick's belt, and in one quick motion threw the blade.

It whistled end over end before embedding itself in the Lectodinian's chest with a solid *thunk*.

Elman clutched at the pommel, his spell fading, his voice gurgling in the darkness as he fell to his knees, then collapsed at Garrick's feet.

Garrick felt the sweet closeness of Will's life force.

This time Braxidane's voice was strong and clear.

... now you must take ...

He was too weak to deny his hunger, too weak to stop himself as he reached out for Will.

But the boy understood instinctively what others could not grasp, and he scuttled away on all fours, tumbling into the brush at the periphery of Garrick's vision.

Good boy, Garrick thought as his hand fell like an iron weight at his side.

"Are you all right?"

The smell of stale pipe tobacco crushed Garrick as another hand drew near. It was Arianna's father, bending over him.

Garrick wanted to tell the man to go away. Perhaps he even managed a grunt. But his hunger was too strong, and his tongue too thick.

Arianna's father touched Garrick's shoulder.

He could not help but drink.

Could not stop himself from feeding his need.

Life force flowed through Garrick, healing his twisted ankle and his burned body. His back arched, drinking deeply. Then he stood and reached for Arianna's brothers.

In an instant, their energy, too, flooded into him.

Then came more. The lives of Lectodinian mages burned as he inhaled them all.

A horrified scream came from the house.

Garrick turned, sensing even more souls. He moved without conscious thought.

Candlelight from the doorway illuminated Arianna's face. Her life force was pure and full, flavored with the familiar scent of strawberry. Her mother stood behind her, her essence robust and warm like the bread she had so often baked.

Take them, his hunger said in an intoxicated rush.

And take them he did, understanding the foul extent of his actions even as he performed them.

There is more, the hunger called.

From inside the house, Garrick sensed the pull of Shayla, Arianna's youngest sister. He clomped through the doorway, struggling against himself with each step. The girl sat on her bed, her expression curious in the dim candlelight.

Take her! The voice inside him cried.

He reached for Shayla, fingers outstretched and yearning. He clenched his eyes and set his jaw. His fists became tight balls.

"No," he groaned and pulled away. *"No."*

Slowly, his rage subsided, and his breathing came into control. Slowly, his surroundings came back into focus.

He ran outside.

The bodies of Arianna and her mother were mere lumps on the porch, her father and brothers a short distance away.

Will sobbed in the distance.

The boy was kneeling beside Kalomar, resting his hand on the horse's flanks.

"Come on, boy," he said in a tiny voice. "You can do it. Get up, boy."

Garrick's heart twisted.

Kalomar was badly burned. Blood glistened from his flank, and a hole as big around as Garrick's fist was burned into the thick muscles of the animal's chest—the same muscles Garrick had marveled at as Kalomar had climbed mountain passes, the same muscles that had flowed so fluidly under him as the horse had carried him across the dry desert of Arderveer.

The animal's proud eyes were still open, but his heart lay motionless inside his chest. Kalomar's ears were pinned back—even in death, nothing could keep him from getting where he was planning to go.

"Can you save him?" Will asked.

His small hand gripped Garrick's arm with firm desperation.

"Save him, Garrick, sir. Save him."

Garrick kneeled to lay a hand on Kalomar's shoulder. He shook his head.

"It's too late," he said. "I'm sorry."

Will threw himself on top of the horse and cried.

"What have I done?" Garrick said. "What have I done?"

"I'll tell you what you've done," a female voice said.

Sunathri stepped from the forest, a thin sword hanging from her hip and a group of Freeborn behind her.

"You've just destroyed the most powerful collection of Lectodinian mages to the east of the desert."

THIRTEEN

Garrick sat alone on a granite boulder in a secluded glade. To the rest of the world, the morning dawned blue and fresh. Across the glade, a patch of clover was green in the blazing sun. Birds called and the summertime breeze rustled through trees. The aroma of wild boar roasting on the Freeborn's spit wafted from the distance.

But for Garrick there was only pain, remorse, and the sense of loss he felt with every turn of the life force inside him.

The feather-thin touch of Arianna's essence seeped through that pool to brush against his chest. She would dissipate soon. Then she would be gone like all the others. He had destroyed her—as he had destroyed her family—yet now she flowed inside him now, so coyly, yet so fully there, reminding him of what a beast he was. But, despite the pain his actions brought him, the life energy also flowed with such strength that he could not deny the glory of the day around him.

It was all such a terrible confusion.

Darien came across the clearing to sit beside him.

"I cannot live like this," Garrick finally said. The words were like bones in his throat.

"I understand."

"You can't possibly understand."

"It was outside your control."

"You're not helping."

Sunathri came to the conversation, sitting to Garrick's left.

"It will come," she said. "Your control will come."

"You don't see their faces," Garrick replied, shaking his head. "You don't feel their lives as you rip them ..."

"You spared the young girl."

"And what a gift I have left for her, eh? To be alone in this world?"

Sunathri placed her hand on his shoulder. Her touch pulled at his life force.

He looked at Will, who stood currying a horse in the distance. He would have to find some way to protect the boy. "You know this isn't finished," he said. "Elman is dead, but the orders will hunt me until it's over."

"Yes, they will," Darien replied.

"I'm going to stop this now."

Darien and Sunathri exchanged hesitant glances.

"What are you saying?" Sunathri said.

"I'm saying I'll not be made a pawn any longer. The planewalkers cannot get away with this. Braxidane cannot make me do this. The orders have god-touched mages. I'm going to find them now. I'm going to confront them. I'm going to end this one way or the other."

"Don't be stupid, Garrick," Darien replied.

"Stupid or not, this needs to happen. This is killing me."

"A confrontation is not as bad of an idea as it might sound," Sunathri said.

"You can't be serious," Darien said.

"Yes, I am. If Garrick can control the confrontation, he might be better off than if he lets the orders set the table. The bigger problem, though, is that I don't think Garrick can get either of their god-touched mages to go anywhere without their armies."

"Like that makes a difference," Darien said.

"It means Garrick needs an army to make his idea happen."

They sat in silence.

"What's your plan, Garrick?" Sunathri said.

"Holy gods, woman," Darien replied. "His plan? His plan? Are you listening to yourself? This is Garrick. He has no *plan*. I mean, beyond calling out to the orders so he can fall face-first on his sword. It's not happening. Garrick is not facing either of the other god-touched mages one-on-one."

"Actually," Garrick said. "I need to face them both at the same time."

Darien threw himself backward on the grass, spreading his arms out wide. "First we can't get you to join us, and now you're off the cliff and talking about combating every mage on the plane at once."

"They don't work well together, Darien. Their approaches are different. Each time I've encountered mixed groups their whole has been less than the sum of their parts. On the other hand, Elman had only Lectodinians in his party, and he nearly destroyed me. I think I stand a better chance one on two than I do if I address them alone."

"All right," Sunathri said again. "What's your plan, Garrick?" Then, interjecting before Darien could reply, "How do you intend to neutralize their god-touched?"

He surprised himself by laughing. He didn't expect Sunathri to treat his idea with such earnest thought.

"I have no plan, but I expect I'll have to draw them out."

"See?" Darien replied, sitting up again.

"We'll want to control the time and place of the meeting," Sunathri said.

"It's too risky," Darien said.

"What isn't?" Sunathri replied. "I say we stop complaining about it and set to helping our friend."

"I'm sorry, Suni," Garrick said. "Darien's right. I can't join the Freeborn."

Sunathri chuckled.

"I really am sorry," Garrick said.

"Don't mistake my laughter, Garrick," Sunathri said. "I'm not asking you to join the Freeborn. I'm saying that if you won't join us, we'll join you."

"I don't understand."

"You mean everything to this House, and we've worked too hard to fail now. You don't have to accept us for us to accept you."

"I'm not telling anyone what to do."

"I'm giving the directions, so you're only taking command if you don't let us help you."

Then it was Garrick's turn to chuckle. "I'm speechless."

"That's not exactly a first," Darien said.

"The Freeborn is not an army, though," Sunathri said. "We can't stand up against two full armies of mercenary men enriched with god-touched wizardry. We'll need help."

She stared at Darien.

"Can you convince your father to support Dorfort joining the fight?"

Darien cleared his throat and shook his head as if contemplating drinking poison before speaking. "I don't know."

"Darien has not spoken to his father in some time," Garrick said.

Sunathri simply stared at him.

"I can try," Darien finally said.

"It's all we can ask," Sunathri replied.

She ran her hand through her thick hair and looked at Garrick. "I think we can name the time and place of your clash—as long as the orders are as serious about getting rid of you as they appear to be."

"How?" Garrick asked.

"You offer yourself as bait—challenge them to a duel neither can turn down without losing face."

"I can see that," Garrick said. "And we choose a place where the god-touched mages have to leave their armies."

"Exactly."

Sunathri's eyes burned with eagerness.

"It could work," Garrick replied.

"Is there such a place?" Darien said.

"Yes," Garrick said. "There is."

Both Sunathri and Darien looked at him.

"God's Tower."

Silence filled the moment.

God's Tower was a solitary snow-capped mountain peak to the south of the Desert of Dust. Alistair had spoken of it on occasion. If legend was true it was the location of the failed council of wizardry that had resulted in the very birth of the orders.

"It's perfect," Sunathri finally said.

Darien raised an eyebrow in contemplation.

"The surrounding land *would* make it difficult for the orders' armies to maneuver. And the tower itself could defend one flank."

"I see just one problem," Garrick said. "How do we contact the orders to make this challenge?"

Sunathri gave a smile. "Leave that to me."

The three paused, and a lightness of being rose inside Garrick. Where once there was nothing, now he saw the outline of a true plan. Where once he felt hopeless, now he felt a camaraderie that he had never felt before.

Darien would work to gather Dorfort's army, Sunathri would wield the Freeborn with her normal aplomb, and Garrick ... Garrick would look the orders' god-touched mages in the eye.

He was no longer a mere apprentice. He was Garrick, god-touched mage of Braxidane.

This would end here.

Sunathri stood up and smoothed her pant leg.

"I think it's time you addressed the Freeborn directly," she said.

"I'll let them know what we are doing, but they will appreciate hearing from you."

Garrick nodded. "I think you're right."

He looked at his friends.

He wasn't alone.

It felt strange. It felt different.

Yes, he thought as both he and Darien stood up. A man has a place he's given and a place he belongs.

Sometimes they're even the same thing.

FOURTEEN

God's Tower was a place of magic, a place of legend, a place of stark, windswept beauty.

Soon it would also be a place of war.

Alistair once told Garrick how Koradic and Lectodine, the two most powerful sorcerers of their time, met there in a council to argue over the control of magic. Those arguments, Alistair said, bore the weight of the schism that birthed the orders.

If Sunathri, Darien, and Garrick had their way, those factions would soon come to God's Tower again, though for how long Garrick could only guess. It was telling about the nature of the human race, he thought, that the only force great enough to bring the Lectodinian and Koradictine orders together was their shared hatred of the independent mages of the Torean Freeborn.

Over the next days, Garrick thought of the tower often during the quiet hours of late evenings and early mornings. He thought about god-touched mages and the open chamber inside the tower. He thought about the devastation of Sjesko, and he remembered blood and mayhem in the depths of Arderveer. The horror of those killing fields would pale in comparison to what was to come.

He thought about the life force that pooled inside him.

It was nearly balanced now.

As long as he kept himself busy he could almost forget the fact that this reservoir had come from Arianna and her family. As long as he could keep himself from remembering too much, he could continue on. But memories were everywhere. They came in aromas that suddenly overwhelmed him, in random images that flashed in his mind so boldly he had to stop what he was doing.

The hunger defined him now. It lay hidden inside, rising late at night to touch his dreams, biding its time. Waiting.

He was god-touched.

His life would never be stable again.

And in those moments when things were at their quietest and when his thoughts turned toward God's Tower, he also thought about the other god-touched mages—those of the Lectodinian and Koradictine orders.

Did they, too, burn with this life force?

Did they carry this same blood lust?

Did they suffer the same way he suffered?

CHAPTER

FIFTEEN

It was early morning as Garrick watched Darien J'ravi, the commander's son, climb atop his horse. Darien's gaze flitted anxiously over the mages who had gathered around him. The day promised to be cloudy, though it appeared rain would stay away. It was early summertime, though, and the heat was already climbing. The ride would be a hot one.

To make matters worse, Darien wore black, befitting his new membership in the Freeborn house. His sleeveless shirt bared his arms and was tucked into a loose-fitting pair of trousers. His leather boots were polished. He had looped a short sword over one shoulder, a weapon that complemented the longer blade he had attached to a saddle loop.

"You don't need to come with me," he said to Garrick.

"You're not getting rid of me that easily," Garrick replied. "We've done nothing but make plans for three weeks now. I feel the need to be doing something."

Darien's grin came from deep within a beard that had grown full. It made him look older.

"That, I understand," he said.

"Beyond that, I may also be able to add weight to the discussion with your father."

Darien nodded but said nothing.

There was no denying the plan hinged on Afarat J'ravi, Darien's father and Commander of the Dorfort guard. Everyone in the Freeborn camp knew it. Darien would ride to Dorfort today, hoping to convince his father to throw the city's defenses against the armies that the orders had already amassed.

Garrick could never fully understand what this mission meant to his friend, but he knew it would come at a cost. Having already lost one son, Afarat J'ravi had blocked Darien's path into the guard. Rather than accept his father's desire, Darien had run off. Though Garrick had traveled with Darien for months, he knew only that Darien's return to Dorfort as a leader of the Freeborn would carry baggage that he couldn't even pretend to guess at. The pressure of soliciting his father's help had to be gnawing at his friend.

"All right, then," Darien finally said. "Let's go."

Garrick smiled, tugged on the cuff of one glove, and climbed onto his horse. It was a brown charger that had been with the Freeborn for many months—it was a good steed, sturdy and dependable, but it felt odd to be without Kalomar.

He wore a blue shirt and a pair of riding breeches that were faded from weeks in the field. His gloves were thin and made of soft leather that fit tight to his hands. Sunathri had offered the black garb of the Freeborn but he refused. Symbols of color were the first vestiges of ownership, and he would not be owned further than he already was.

"Will!" Garrick called to the boy.

Will came to his side. His sunken eyes and unkempt hair told of fitful sleep.

Garrick wanted to talk to Will because the boy's confidence and sense of joy were flagging. Will knew something big was happening, even if he couldn't figure out exactly what it was. Garrick was leaving him alone too long—and Will was missing Kalomar even more than

Garrick did. In the horse's death, Will had lost a home. It was a feeling Garrick understood.

Garrick leaned over his steed's neck. "I'm going into Dorfort with Darien."

"Can I come along?" Will asked.

"No," Garrick said. "But I will be back soon."

"Promise?"

"Yes, I promise. I need you to look out for Suni. Help her where you can, all right?"

The boy drew a sigh and nodded as if giving himself strength.

"All right," Will said. "I'll look after Miss Suni for you."

"I'm counting on you," Garrick said, tousling the boy's hair. Then Garrick sat up in his saddle and smiled. It *did* feel good to be doing something for a change.

"Come on, Darien, what are you waiting for?" he said.

Darien spurred his horse on, and the two headed for their meeting with Afarat J'ravi, Commander of the Dorfort guard, and Darien's father.

It was time to gather their army.

SIXTEEN

The reception from the people of Dorfort was not particularly warm, but it gave Garrick a sense of comfort to realize he no longer cared.

His life force was strong enough that he felt the city as he and Darien proceeded over streets that dry weather had turned into ribbons of hard-packed, reddish clay. The town was in full mid-morning churn, but he felt everything as it moved around him. An essence of concern permeated the city, sticky and tasting bitterly of angst. It reeked of possible magewar. And amidst that concern, he sensed the edge of distrust brought on by rumors of Garrick's own sorcery, distrust that was caustic and carried the faint smell of distant lightning.

Whispers came as they passed, though he could not say if the whispers were real, or were merely fearful sighs caught in the web of his god-touched magic.

There was no doubt, however, that the people of this city were anxious and wary. News of the Freeborn's arrival had preceded them. The citizens of Dorfort knew why Darien and Garrick were here, and they didn't agree the quest was needed. The Freeborn's concern was a squabble between mages, they said. It had no effect on the world as they knew it.

Garrick understood better, though. The citizens of Dorfort may not see the truth properly, but that didn't change that truth. And the truth of the day was that two armies of mages, each led by god-touched wizards, were preparing to sweep across the plane of Adruin. This truth—and the fact he was hot and uncomfortable from the ride—were the only things that bothered him right now.

Did that mean he was growing up?

Perhaps.

But rather than worry about it, he spent his time thinking about the task.

Darien had been quiet throughout the morning—something out of character. The air of disdain the city held for them seemed to bother Darien more than it bothered Garrick. He looked downright grim and spent most of the trip chewing the inside of his cheeks and glancing up into the sky.

Of course, everything in the Freeborn's plan depended on the argument Darien would make to his father this morning. Without Dorfort's might behind them, Garrick and the Freeborn would fail. The pressure had to be intense.

"I never knew my father," Garrick said, hoping to find something to keep Darien's mind occupied.

Darien gave him a sideways glance.

"I don't know what it's like to live in a shadow like that," Garrick continued. "But I do know what it's like to be seen as an apprentice in a world of mages. Perhaps it's similar to what you're working through today?"

"What are you saying, Garrick?"

He shrugged.

"I always feel ... incompetent ... when I'm around real sorcerers. Like they've done so much more than I have. They always seem to know so much more, seem to be so comfortable." Garrick waited a moment. "But things, they seem to happen however they were fated to."

Darien laughed, and Garrick felt better.

"I'm not worried my father will think me incompetent."

"What are you worried about, then?"

"I've gone against his wishes."

"So you think you've let him down?"

"Maybe."

"You think he'll be angry."

They traveled farther without speaking.

"No," Darien said. "That's not it."

"So, what is it?"

"I don't know."

"I see," Garrick replied, though he most definitely did not see.

"What if he doesn't even grant me an audience?" Darien finally said.

Garrick grunted in return.

"He *will* be angry," Darien said. "It's certainly possible he won't want to see me."

"Your father loves you, Darien."

"No. My father loved the boy I was. I have no idea what he thinks of me now."

Garrick brought a gloved hand up to scratch the side of his cheek. "Well," he said. "I suppose we could just skip it all. Just head back to Caledena, hit the Dragongriff tables again, and put it all on Griffin five."

Darien laughed again.

"Only if you use your sorcery right and proper this time."

"You drive a hard bargain."

A short while later they came to their destination.

The wall surrounding Dorfort's government center was impressive, a thick and impervious barricade made of mortar and stone. Heavy oaken doors blocked the entrance, and guards stood between crenellations at the top of the wall. The university center, brilliant in its whitewashed splendor, rose to the sky to Garrick's right, and a granary complete with its water-driven millstone was built to his left.

Garrick had spent hours at the university center over the past weeks. He had picked through hundreds of scrolls and diaries that were filled with musty ruminations made about the orders. Yet, he didn't feel any wiser for them.

Their horses approached the gate.

"Greetings, Harol," Darien called to the guard.

"Darien," Harol replied. "It has been too long."

"I need to see my father."

"With whom do you ride?"

"This is Garrick, a Torean mage. I vouch he has no ill intentions."

"Aye," Harol said. "Your word is good."

The door rumbled and creaked open with the strained sound of taut rope.

Darien gave the guard his weapons, and Garrick promptly did the same. After stable workers took their mounts, they followed Harol as he escorted them across the manor yard and toward the inner castle. Women stopped their washing as Garrick and Darien passed. A young boy tending goats leaned on his staff to stare at them. Guards watched their every step.

It was Darien they were looking at, Garrick realized.

"You've created quite a stir," he said.

"Yes," Darien replied. "It's not every day that the commander's boy comes home with a demon mage in tow."

Their boots rang out against the stone walkway.

As they approached the central manor, the door swung open to reveal an old man, draped in blue robes, standing in shadow. He was tall, with silvery gray hair that swirled around his head. His eyes were the same green as Darien's. His body was aged, but still carried a heft that spoke of his robust youth.

The man took a breath. "Darien," he said.

"Father," Darien replied.

Garrick's heart pounded as Darien and his father stood apart. For a moment he thought either of them might turn away. Instead, Commander J'ravi stepped forward and they embraced.

"You must be Garrick," the elder man said.

"Yes," Garrick replied as he clasped the commander's extended hand. Despite J'ravi's age, the grip was firm and dry.

"Come in, then," Afarat J'ravi said, guiding them through the doorway. "Let's have a talk."

Darien walked with easy steps beside his father, and Garrick followed. The hallway was lined with swaths of colored cloth, and the floor was padded with rugs. The commander led them to a comfortable room where sunlight streamed through an open window. A tray of bread sat on a small table—overflowing with thick cuts of ryes, wheats, and barleys that smelled good.

Darien tore off a piece as they sat down.

The commander's lips looked as if they were permanently too dry. He licked them and peered at his son.

"Wine?" the commander offered.

"No, Father. We cannot stay long."

"I assumed as much."

Garrick felt suddenly out of place.

"I heard you had left the university," the commander said. "But I didn't realize you had aligned with the Toreans."

"We need your help," Darien said.

The elder J'ravi shook his head gently. "I've always found that meddling in sorcerous concerns is better left to the wizards."

"In this case, Father, the concerns of those sorcerers bleed into those of the rest of the plane. You know that, don't you? The orders will turn their attention to the rest of the plane when they are finished with the Toreans."

The commander stood and walked to the window.

"Our scouts suggest as much, but I'm not sure how much trust to put in them."

Darien came to stand beside his father.

"Your scouts speak true."

The commander raised a questioning eyebrow.

"It's time to do something."

"I don't know, Darien," his father replied. "Dorfort has shed so much of its young blood. How much of that has been necessary? Do you *really* know how deep the effects of war can be? Do you know how many lives we have given in efforts that gained us nothing?"

Darien sighed, then replied in a low voice.

"Sometimes I remember the way Thale would stomp around this place and demand everyone within earshot listen to him. You remember that, too, don't you?"

"He was always the emotional one," Commander J'ravi replied.

"Yes. And people loved him for it."

His father nodded.

"I used to hate him, though," Darien said.

The commander's face darkened.

"I hated him because everyone else loved him, and I knew I

could never match him. He was so perfect. Bigger than life, you know? And as he grew up I hated him because he put his beliefs before us—because he felt them so strongly he was willing to die for them. I thought that was terribly selfish, and I hated him even more for it."

"What is your point, Darien?"

"I understand him now, and you do, too. There are times when risks must be taken. Thale *had* to do what he did or he would not have been Thale."

"No." The old commander's eyes grew vacant. "Thale died because I signed the battle order."

"Thale died because he believed in what he spoke of. It was his choice, and it was the right one. Just like mine is to fight against the orders."

The commander walked from the window and took his seat. Only then did Garrick notice his limp. Afarat J'ravi had been a soldier his whole life, but now he was a soldier grown old.

"Has war ever accomplished anything?" he said.

Darien gestured outside.

"Look at this city for your answer, Father. Think of the dangers this city has faced, the evils you've fought. These people would not be living in peace without the decisions you've made. This city is what that bloodshed has accomplished."

The commander stared at Darien for long enough that Garrick grew uncomfortable.

"I have been a foolish old man," he finally said, "holding so tightly to my dead son that I could not let loose of the one that lived. I am sorry, Darien."

Darien put his hand on his father's forearm.

Garrick sensed the sense of purpose that drove Darien crash against the pillar of strength Afarat J'ravi had built over the entirety of his life, and Garrick realized Darien had become a man in the eyes of his father today. The realization made him jealous.

"We need Lord Ellesadil to throw his lot in with the Freeborn,"

Darien said. "If we don't stop the orders now, they will roll over the rest of Adruin before it is done."

Commander J'ravi sighed. "You feel this fully, then? There will be magewar?"

"Magewar is already being fought, sir," Garrick interrupted with more vitriol than he meant.

"What Garrick means," Darien said, "is that the Torean House has already been destroyed on the western half of the plane, and it's likely that raids of the springtime have killed most of the powerful Toreans in the eastern regions, too."

Darien's father sipped wine from his goblet and seemed to find a new strength.

"The orders have always skirmished without causing problems outside their ranks. Why should this be different?"

"The orders have god-touched mages," Darien said, glancing at Garrick. "*All* of the orders do."

Commander J'ravi turned to Garrick. "So that rumor is true, also."

Garrick nodded.

"I need your help, Father. The armies of the orders are strong and dangerously unpredictable. We are going to confront their god-touched mages directly—or at least Garrick will. But we need your help to convince Lord Ellesadil to send an army of Dorfort's guard to accompany us."

"It sounds like a suicide mission."

The commander looked at Garrick then, his eyes piercing with an unspoken question.

How? He was asking. *How will you deal with mages who are more powerful than you? Why should I think you can do this?* The questions lay like acid in Garrick's stomach. The answers boiled up through his life force, and he found he had to take a breath before he spoke.

"We have a plan," Garrick said.

"A plan." The commander chuckled. "There is always a plan." He sat back in his chair and took another quick sip of his wine. "All right," he said. "Let me hear of this plan."

EIGHTEEN

Everything happened quickly.

Commander J'ravi held a session with Lord Ellesadil.

Then the commander met with advanced scouts and gathered his sergeants and staff together to work on a plan. Ellesadil sought Torean council from the outside, but couldn't find any beyond the Freeborn—a fact that Afarat J'ravi ensured Dorfort's leader couldn't miss seeing as proof of the orders' intentions. Then, after a final flurry of review, Commander J'ravi brought the issue to a head by pressing Ellesadil for an answer.

His timing was impeccable.

Dorfort's leader agreed not only to give them an entire division of the guard, but also to dispatch messengers to nearby towns to enlist as much aid as possible.

Afarat J'ravi had been magnificent. It was unusual to find a man who spoke from the heart and was still such a remarkable politician. And, as Garrick watched the commander work, he realized exactly how much of the man he saw in Darien.

"It's time to hail the orders," Sunathri said as she laid out components for her spell. "Are you ready?"

It was nearly evening, and a lazy rain pattered against the tent's taut covering. The idea of speaking directly to the orders' superior mages made Garrick's stomach churn, but Sunathri was right. It was time.

"I'm ready," Garrick replied. "Talk me through the process, though. I want to learn."

Sunathri gave one of her coy smiles. "I would have expected your new superior to teach you these things," she said.

"Just teach me how to do this," he said.

"I'll do my best."

She placed powdered chalk into a brazier and gave Garrick a stick of vermillion grease. "Draw a triangle around the brazier. Make it thick. Then pour the water."

He drew the diagram.

Sunathri retrieved a bottle from her footlocker. "Each point in the triangle represents a member of the conversation. The chalk acts as the medium. The lines between each point ensure we're each connected."

"It seems a powerful sorcery."

"It is, but the strongest spells often require the least amount of energy."

"Alistair often said that."

"People think sorcery is about power. But the strongest magics, the more sophisticated ones, depend on your pattern of thought more than they depend on the energy itself. Once you understand what you're trying to accomplish, the complexities fade and you can feel every detail of the spell—which makes your castings more efficient."

"That makes sense. In a strange way."

"Yes, it's a conundrum. Simple spells succeed without clarity of thought. So they can become so familiar that you cast them by rote rather than with any crispness or strength of thought."

"I see," Garrick said.

As he thought back, it did make sense.

Ripping life force and casting bolts of magic were both simple works in the end—but they took up incredible energy, while the complex illusion he cast to evade Elman outside Caledena hadn't cost him as dearly as he had expected.

Sunathri unstopped a bottle and the aroma of strong mint filled the air. She placed three drops into the brazier, each blotting up green in the chalk.

"What's that for?" Garrick asked.

"Just a little something to make the conversation pleasant."

"Hmmm."

"You can learn the basics of magic from anyone, but eventually you have to make it your own."

"Alistair used to say something like that, too."

"Maybe those are the things that make our orders so different. Lectodinians believe in control, and structure. They conform to standards while the Koradictines' work is based on raw consumption above all else. Once you understand that, you can see why the two of them struggle to get along. A Lectodinian sees magic as a limited resource and the act of casting to be almost a form of art in itself, while a Koradictine sees magic as if it flows from Talin in a boundless stream that is to be wallowed in."

"And, of course, a Torean would prefer to just ignore it all," Garrick added.

"Indeed. We stand on our own. Why should our magic be controlled by anyone else? Of course, that causes its own problems."

Garrick shrugged.

"All right. We're ready," she said. "Go to the other side of the table and take my hands."

Her fingers were cold to the touch.

"As the process moves, I want you to let your thoughts flow into mine. Listen to the conversation, and funnel your energy so it aids me. If you do it right, neither of the superiors will know you're here with me."

"All right."

Suni closed her eyes, and Garrick did likewise.

Sunathri spoke her magic in a melodious voice.

Garrick set gates, opened a link to the plane of magic, and let his magestuff slip into her spell. A pattern formed in his head. He felt the power of her concentration and sensed its order.

"Hail, Koradictine," she said. "Hail, Lectodinian."

The chalk flared with white light, and a face appeared in the liquid surface of the brazier.

"Greetings, *Torean*."

The voice was unearthly, yet human. As a face appeared in one brazier, Garrick knew immediately that it belonged to Zutrian Esta, the mage superior of the Lectodinian order.

"To what do we owe this unexpected pleasure?"

"I'm sure," a second voice chimed in—this one Ettril Dor-Entfar, leader of the Koradictines—"that I speak for my Lectodinian friend when I say we have better things to do."

"I am Sunathri Katella," Sunathri said. "Lord Superior of the Torean House of the Freeborn."

Zutrian's voice rose to a chuckle. "I had no idea such a collective existed."

"Please don't feel the need to be so purposefully dull on my account," Sunathri replied. "The entire plane knows you're hunting Toreans because of the Freeborn."

"What is it you want?" Ettril gave a curt reply.

"I have a proposal."

"Another first," Zutrian said.

"You have expended great effort to find and destroy our god-touched mage, yet Garrick still lives."

The Koradictine's eyebrow rose with interest.

"Tell us of your proposal, Mage Superior," Zutrian snarled.

Garrick felt Sunathri's demeanor change, and he couldn't help but feel pleasure at the superiors' discomfort.

"Choose the strongest of your god-touched wizards," she said. "And pit him directly against ours. If Garrick wins, the orders leave us alone. If he loses, we disband the Freeborn."

"And why should we do that?" Ettril replied.

"A very good question," Zutrian added. "It's just as easy to carve your territory up a bit at a time."

"All that accomplishes is to provide you each more time to plot against the other. If you both prefer to hide your heads in the sand until the other double-crosses you, I suppose it is none of my concern. But my proposal still stands."

"You speak brashly, Sunathri Katella, Lord Superior of the Tore-ans," Zutrian said.

"Perhaps. But the fact is that neither of you can be certain of controlling the plane while Garrick lives, and you both know that no collection of normal mages will be able to stop him."

The two superiors waited.

"You lost dozens of mages at Arderveer alone, and more in both Caledena and Dorfort. Your approach may well cripple the Torean order, but we can fight like this for many years, taking a few mages here and a few there, hindering your progress at every turn. When Garrick aligns with our ranks, you will not be able to stop us. And as his legend grows, more mages *will* join us. You know this is true. And you know the game we offer is the best opportunity you'll ever get to deal with the issue."

"And, pray tell, what might the Toreans get out of this proposal of yours?" Ettril said.

"When Garrick defeats your champion, you will agree to leave us alone. We get a quiet place in the power structure of the plane, a place we can live as we wish."

Both the superiors smiled.

Ettril ran his fingers through his beard. "What say you, Zutrian? Do we close out this business with the Toreans now, or do we opt for the drawn-out affair that the Torean predicts?"

"If the Freeborn wants to die quickly," Zutrian said. "I see no reason not to accommodate them."

"My thoughts exactly," the Koradictine replied.

"Then the next step is for the two of you to select a champion," Sunathri said.

Ettril Dor-Entfar spoke first, "I will send Jormar to destroy the Torean god-touched."

"The Koradictine approach failed in Arderveer," Zutrian replied. "I suggest the Lectodinian, Parathay, should be our representative this time."

"Arderveer has nothing to do with this."

"Arderveer has everything to do with it," Zutrian snipped.

"You say this," Ettril replied sharply, "And, yet, from what I hear your Lectodinians could not stop Garrick in Caledena or Dorfort, either."

The conversation fell silent for the barest of moments. Garrick sensed Suni's satisfaction rise. It had gone exactly as she anticipated, and he felt something strong stirring inside her. A sense of power came over him that was deeper than magic, deeper than the hunger that thrummed from Braxidane's curse. It was connection to the moment, a sense of knowing exactly where he was and exactly why he was here.

It was time to do his part.

"Send them both," Garrick said, enjoying the shocked expressions of both superiors.

"Garrick," Zutrian said, smiling sickly as he recovered from his surprise. "So we finally meet."

"Send them both," Garrick repeated. "I care not."

"That would make it easier," Ettril replied.

"Excellent," said Suni. "Then both it is. Garrick will be at the top of God's Tower in two weeks' time."

"I will not overstress my army merely to meet a Torean wizard," Ettril replied. "I will need a month."

"Yes, a month sounds more proper," Zutrian said.

"A month it is, then," Suni said. "We will see you there."

Then she broke the link. Thin wisps of steam rose from the brazier's surface, chalk smoldered with a coarse reek, and the lines between the three points were now obliterated.

Garrick still held Sunathri's hands. The contact seemed suddenly intimate, and Garrick felt heat rise to his face. He pulled his hands away.

"Well, that's done," Sunathri said as if she hadn't noticed their closeness.

"They seemed less than worried," Garrick replied.

"Which is exactly how we want them."

CHAPTER

TWENTY

Lord Ellesadil and his family came to see the army off. They sat in the shade on a platform along the gathering field as soldiers, several thousand strong, mustered at the bank of Blue Lake. It was morning, still early enough that the grass was damp and the sun's shadows still slanted at sharp angles across the glade.

An air of anticipation clung to the field that Garrick had no need of life force to feel.

He wore leather breeches, a shirt of green cloth, and a black bandana that looped around his neck. His hair blew in the wind. He had just finished rolling his travel kit together when a guard approached, clearly nervous about speaking with him.

"The royal family would like a word," the guard said.

Garrick glanced at Sunathri, who shrugged.

"Thank you," he replied. "I'll come to the box immediately."

The man turned to leave, but Garrick placed a hand on the man's shoulder and the man looked at him with unconcealed fear. This soldier was a simple man, doing his job. But he was afraid this might be the last day he saw his home and his family, and he was afraid of Garrick in ways he could not express.

"Go well today, sir," Garrick said.

The man's smile of relief was all Garrick needed to see.

"Thank you, Lord Garrick."

"Just call me Garrick. We both know I am no lord."

"Indeed, sir. That I will."

Garrick grinned as the man left. News of this encounter would be passed around the ranks in rapid fashion. It was something Darien would have done.

"We'll make a leader of you yet," Sunathri said with her most mischievous smile.

Garrick grumbled, but he liked the idea that she had noticed.

"Why would Lord Ellesadil want to speak with me?"

"Are you being dense on purpose?"

"No."

Sunathri smirked. "The lord wishes to see you because he knows you are the key to victory. And he wants to see you *now* because he wants the members of his army to see him with you. He will use your promise to enhance his image. You need to learn to take advantage of that."

He glanced at Will—who was grooming Garrick's horse with a sense of detachment.

"Can you watch him?"

"Of course."

Garrick weaved his way through the Dorfort guard as they bent to sharpen their swords and daggers, as they tested bows and prepared their travel kits, and as they attended to their animals. Families huddled by their husbands, fathers, wives, and daughters.

Which ones would not make it back?

Which of these families would lose loved ones because of his decision to face down the orders?

The thought struck him like cold water to his face.

He tried to ignore comments as he went, but the people of

Dorfort were hard to ignore. He sensed both curiosity and fear. They didn't understand him. They didn't trust him. They thought this war of Darien's was a simple skirmish between mages that would soon blow over. A few even felt this was all Garrick's doing, that he had enspelled Darien to bring him to his sway. These people thought everyone would be safe so long as the politicians stayed out of it. Yet, these same people were preparing to fight, regardless.

That was all because of Ellesadil, of course.

The lord had a calmness about him, a sense of control that gave people reason to follow. Despite fears and doubts, they trusted Ellesadil. They believed in him. If the lord said it was important that they place their lives at risk, then it was important.

Garrick arrived at Ellesadil's platform.

The lord stood under the observation canopy, before a large chair. He wore a blue tunic edged with silver thread. A riding cape, its fabric dyed goldenrod yellow, hung from the back of his seat. Fine lines at the corners of his eyes said he was older than the rest of his appearance suggested. Those eyes were brown and his gaze steady. His curly dark hair had a few strands of gray running through it.

Lady Ellesadil remained seated in the shade, resplendent in her green dress with golden trim. Rings gleamed from her fingers, and a jeweled necklace clung to the hollow of her throat.

The fineness of the royal couple's wardrobe seemed out of place in the middle of the glade.

The lord came to stand before Garrick.

"Go with fortune," he said.

"Thank you, Lord."

"I have met often with my new captain," Ellesadil motioned across the field to Darien, "yet, you and I have not had the opportunity to speak. I wanted to provide you my blessings and also make certain you understood the arrangements."

"I understand the arrangement. Darien leads your army."

"Do you truly understand?" Ellesadil replied. "Do you feel how the people of my realm are uncertain whether a magewar is something our warriors should die for?"

"Yes," he replied. "I do feel that. And I understand how unpopular your decision will be if this plan does not succeed. But I also know you understand the true dangers the orders pose, and that you would never have participated if that wasn't so."

Ellesadil's gaze was sharp. "Still, I wouldn't be throwing my lot with *your* order if I did not retain full control of the effort."

"It's not my order."

"Not yet."

Suddenly, Garrick understood the real purpose of this discussion.

"You've chosen well, Lord Ellesadil. Darien and I have traveled together for some time. He is a fine man. And Sunathri is the right choice to lead the Freeborn. To put this as boldly as I can, I have no aspirations to displace either of them, even if you asked me to."

Ellesadil smiled warmly.

"Then you are a wiser man than I am," Ellesadil said with a smile that felt forced.

Garrick laughed but felt awkward at the same time. "Thank you, I think." He glanced over the field that was filled with soldiers. "It appears we are nearing the point where we are ready to leave," he said.

"Go with my blessing, then," Ellesadil said, extending his hand.

Garrick took it.

WILL WAS STILL GROOMING his horse when Garrick returned. The boy's face was dark with forced concentration. It was an expression that hurt Garrick. This was going to be a hard conversation. Will had, after all, saved his life when Elman had attacked in the woods outside Arianna's home. He would not be happy.

A battlefield was no place for a boy, though.

Garrick knew what he needed to do.

On his mount, Darien drew close, his father riding alongside him. In addition to the black garb of the Freeborn, Darien wore a silver helm with a crest of red feathers that ran from front to back. His shoulder plates and thigh buckles carried the seal of the city and his shield was painted with two golden slashes that marked him as field commander.

"Are you ready to start?" Darien asked.

"Nearly," Garrick replied. "Commander J'ravi, I need your help."

"How can I serve?" Darien's father responded.

"I need you to take care of the boy until I return."

"No!" Will cried, wrapping his arms around Garrick's waist. "I'm coming with you."

Garrick bent to look Will in the eye. "It's too dangerous, Will."

"I want to come."

"You're too young for this trip."

"No, I'm not! I look out for you! If it weren't for me, you would already be dead by now."

Garrick pursed his lips.

"A battlefield is different. You're a smart boy. You know this is true."

Tears came to Will's eyes, but the boy fought them back. "You'll come back, won't you?"

Garrick nodded.

"Promise?"

Will's gaze was intense. He was no more than twelve, but he knew things about life that a boy his age shouldn't know. He knew adults lied sometimes, but he also knew Garrick had kept his promises before.

"I'll never lie to you, Will. That means I'll only promise what I can. And because I don't know what will happen at God's Tower, I'll only promise to return if I'm able." And he would, too. He liked Will. The boy made him feel good. Will seemed somehow important, and Garrick wanted to make Will's life better than Garrick's had been.

Will embraced him with a hug. "Be careful," he whispered.

The commander gave a wide smile. "I think we can manage to keep young Will occupied. I've missed having a boy around."

"Thank you," Garrick said.

He mounted his horse and straightened himself. Sunathri was already prepared. Her horse blew an anxious snort.

"Trumpeter," Darien said. "Blow the march!"

The trumpeter raised his instrument then and blew a clear signal to the men. Voices rose in a throaty cheer. Chains rattled, leather creaked, and the march to God's Tower began.

TWENTY-ONE

Traveling with an army was different from traveling alone. Rather than being concerned with predators or thieves, the days were filled with problems of simple logistics and gargantuan tempers. There were rumors about the Lectodinian army and more tales of the Koradictine. Each day brought some perceived contact with one of their spies or scouts, generally in the form of a days-old camp with its cold firepit.

Nothing of substance, though.

The triviality of it wore Garrick down. These things were meaningless when compared to the truth of what was to come. He found himself whiling time by mindlessly setting gates and running pinches of life force through them. He drew patterns in his horse's coat and dripped magic into those patterns, changing the fur's color, texture, and length before returning it to its natural state. It was a waste of energy, but he couldn't help it.

As an experiment, he pushed life force up through his arm and into his hand. His index finger grew a new knuckle, and he was so astonished he nearly fell off his horse.

"Are you okay, Lord?" a man asked.

"Yes," he said as he hid his hand. "I'm fine."

It took him the better part of the afternoon to fix his error.

THE PLAN WAS THIS:

He would use his hunger.

He would starve himself, and he would enter God's Tower prepared to use Braxidane's curse to his favor.

The idea weighed hard on him. It felt … wrong. Using his hunger as a weapon made him feel dark and cold. Like he was nothing but a blade, nothing more than a piece of steel to be smelted and fired and honed and made to carry an edge that would bite indiscriminately. The stark audacity of the plan made him feel cold. It's ruthlessness made him feel hollow. Made him feel ugly.

But that was the plan, empty his vessel as far as he could and use the black side of himself to rip the souls from the Lectodinian and Koradictine mages.

Would that work against other god-touched mages?

He didn't know.

But his only alternative was to arrive at God's Tower bloated and ready to cast stronger magic than he had ever before attempted—and he could not accept the idea of sacrificing an entire village, or an entire army, as it might be, to reap the life force he would need to support that plan. And, in his heart, even if Garrick could have managed the burden of such a mass sacrifice, he wasn't sure he could defeat the orders' god-touched mages in a battle of pure sorcery, anyway.

But what did it say about him that he was willing to set himself up to trigger his own rampage?

He didn't want to think about it.

But he couldn't help it. He *had* to think about it.

He had to manage himself carefully if this whole thing was going to work. He had to stay strong enough to make it to the tower without bowing to his hunger's desire to feed, and still arrive there weak enough to steal the other god-touched mages' energy. It was a difficult equation to balance.

He went to his bedroll each night more drained than he had been the night before. Each morning he found it more difficult to rise, and each day he felt his hunger growing stronger as the sun moved across the sky. He fought it constantly, keeping its tendrils from drifting out among the men and women of the Torean army. He breathed it down, feeling its aroma and its pull growing stronger with time.

As his reservoir faded, he stopped his mindless practicing and merely sat quietly in his saddle. In the evenings he squatted in meditation, trying to conserve as much of himself as he could. The ranks watched him intently as they traveled, whispering more and more about the sense of isolation he was emoting. They understood all too well his part of their effort and they were growing worried.

Not that he blamed them.

A few days later, the Torean army drew near enough to God's Tower that they could see its peak gleaming white in the distance. Their arrival served to make Garrick even more irritable.

THE MORNING before they were to make their final camp, Sunathri came to Garrick's tent. He stirred but did not rise. He could see God's Tower in the distance through the open flap, its peak blazing in the early sun.

He rose to sit as Sunathri came to the edge of his cot and put her hand above his knee. The heat of her fingers stirred his hunger through the thin fabric of the sheet. She tasted of confidence and passion. He felt her heartbeat and wanted to be closer to it, but he had learned more about fighting this desire of his and he was able to dispel it far enough to concentrate on her.

"You are weak," she said.

"I'm just waking up."

"You know what I mean. Your life force wanes."

"Then the plan is working," he joked.

"Stop it," Sunathri replied. "You need something. Everyone can see it. You can't make it up the mountainside like this."

Garrick nodded, surprised to have to fight hunger again. Suni was right. He would feed soon regardless of his efforts. He shrugged. "Maybe so. All I can say for sure is that Braxidane's curse does not much appreciate its cage."

"Take me," she said.

"What?" He grimaced.

"Use my life force to defeat the orders."

He felt the horror of her idea etch its way up his face. "I'm not going to kill you, Sunathri."

"It will be worth it. If you don't feed soon, our entire quest is doomed. You need this, Garrick. Why not take one who fully chooses to go?"

Her grip grew firmer on his knee, and he felt each of her fingers. Did he love her? How could he know? What was love? All he could say for sure was that she was beautiful, that he did not want her to leave, and that suddenly his words would not flow.

"I can't," he said.

She moved even closer. He felt her nearness as a painful, glorious pressure.

"No!" He pushed her so hard she fell off his cot.

She hesitated, then stood and walked to the opening of his tent. "Then we are lost," she said.

She left the flap free to flutter in the morning breeze.

TWENTY-TWO

God's Tower rose like a sentry above them, a massive peak of white, brown, and green that seemed to be chiseled into the sky. As planned, they arrived days before the confrontation.

The Dorfort guard set about immediately to prepare the land, digging trenches and setting pike traps. They built platforms for their archers, and bunkers for their foot soldiers.

Darien commanded nearly five thousand of them, and Sunathri claimed over a hundred wizards. But these would pale against the numbers the orders would bring. Their scouts had spotted spies from the Koradictine and Lectodinian camps throughout their march, so Darien and Sunathri assumed the orders were aware of their numbers—in fact, their deception relied upon it.

Suni split her sorcerers into three groups.

Under cover of darkness, two smaller teams of twenty-five mages looped around the mountain to position themselves in locations where they could hide away, the goal being that each would slip behind the orders' armies and attack to create disarray. To support this maneuver, Darien asked for volunteers among the warriors to be outfitted in black—one for each of the mages that left the main force. It was a dangerous duty because the Torean mages would be the orders' obvious first targets, but volunteers were found.

Garrick had little to do but appear confident for the benefit of the army, and to dwell upon his upcoming battle. He was tired, so drained he could barely move, so exhausted from fighting his hunger that he was beginning to lose track of events. He still had no plan for his confrontation beyond forcing the two other god-touched mages to work together. So Garrick spent his days hiding away and fighting the anxiety that built with each passing moment.

He was ready to have this over with.

THE SKY WAS overcast and the clouds were darkening as the evening faded toward nighttime. Garrick, Darien, and Sunathri sat before a warm fire that cast orange fingers across the clearing.

It would all begin tomorrow.

Garrick sat stoically, bracing himself against the burning need to rip energy from everything that moved, and listening to the echoes of Braxidane's amused laughter clutter his mind. He was so close, he thought—so close to losing everything. No one else knew the depths of this pain. How could they? He was more alone than anyone could know. He was a solitary island of corruption in a sea of humanity.

"It's time to put our plans into action," Darien said.

Sunathri nodded. She looked tired, her gaze oddly indifferent, mesmerized by the flame of their fire. It had been a long and stressful trip. Preparations had taken much from her.

"Our mages should be in place behind the orders' lines by morning," she finally said.

Garrick smiled with the corner of one lip. He and Sunathri had not been alone since she offered herself to him. She had been distant and aloof since then. The flavor of her rejection was sharp and bitter.

"I've assigned roles and we've run our practices," Darien added. "Tomorrow we'll have fifty warriors cloaked in Torean black. They know what is expected of them."

"Everything sounds good," Garrick replied.

An awkward silence ensued. The fire crackled.

Sunathri chewed a piece of dried meat.

Darien's gaze flitted to Sunathri and back again, the unspoken communication between them clear.

"I am concerned for you, Garrick," Darien finally said.

"Why is that?"

"You need to be agile and quick-witted to face the orders' god-touched mages. But I've seen you like this before. You are too weak. I think it bodes poorly."

"I'll be fine," Garrick said.

"Perhaps. But, as a commander of this army, it worries me that one of my weapons is unreliable."

"Is that what I am to you, Darien? A weapon?"

Darien glared at him. "Be reasonable, Garrick. You do realize that everything depends on you being at your best tomorrow, right?"

"I said I'll be fine."

The curtness of his response created more silence during which the intensity of Darien's gaze was like an anvil pressing down on him.

"What do you want me to say, Darien? That the hunger is intense now. Is that it? That it eats at my soul. Is that what you want to hear? Because, if so, then let me tell you all of that is true. Let me say that it burns and aches, let me tell you that if I let this hunger free this very moment, I could reach out and destroy you all."

The fire crackled.

"Is that what you wanted to hear?"

Darien sighed and rubbed his eyes. The past weeks had been hard on him, too. "I'm sorry Garrick. I truly am. If anyone understands your plight, it's me. But you asked for this mission, and I command an army of people who have put their lives at stake for you. What I want to hear—what they want to hear—is that you are capable of doing your part. And to be abundantly clear, I don't see how you will make it up the hill tomorrow when you can barely manage to roll out of bed as it is."

"I'll manage."

"How?"

Garrick felt Sunathri's stare as a weight, but ignored her.

"There is no other choice."

Darien nodded. Sunathri said nothing. The fire still crackled, and Garrick felt the eyes of the world falling on his shoulders like a hard, pelting rain. He took a deep breath to clear his ache, and he rolled his neck around on his shoulders.

"All right," Darien said, standing up. "I trust you. I'm going to see to my army, then retire for the night. Sentries are set. Preparations will start in earnest before the sun rises."

"Good night, Darien," Sunathri said.

Darien glanced at her as he left. If Garrick hadn't been paying attention, he might have missed her returning his expression with a nod that was so subtle he wondered if he imagined it. But he felt it in his hunger, too. It was a nod that carried a sense of finality.

It took all of his conscious thought to maintain his composure.

Were his friends conspiring against him?

He did not like the feeling of being so paranoid.

A breeze blew strands of Sunathri's black hair into her face. She reached up and brushed them away, then used a stick to prod the fire. The sound of the camp echoed dimly in the distance.

"The mages are speaking among themselves," she said.

"What are they saying?"

"They say we are lovers, and that you have spurned me. They say that is why I am so angry."

"I'm sorry," Garrick said.

"I'm the one who should be sorry. It was wrong to put you in that position. When we communed to contact the orders, our link was strong and clear. I knew then what you felt for me, but still I asked you to take my life. That was unkind of me."

"I'm sorry I couldn't do it," he said.

"It's all right."

She moved close and turned his head toward her with one hand. Slowly, she leaned forward.

He felt her lips against his, gentle and unencumbered by anything but the moment. His hunger surged forward, and he found himself clenching a fist in his struggle to keep control. They broke the contact, and Garrick looked at her. Firelight reflected off her features. She had always been attractive, but tonight she was truly the most beautiful person he had ever seen.

"You've seen what happens to those who love me."

"You're learning control. I have faith in you."

"I wish I was as certain."

She smiled and stood. "I should go. We both need our rest."

He nodded. "Good night."

"Good night," she replied, then disappeared into the night.

He sat silently, thinking about her words.

Was she right? Was he gaining control?

Perhaps it didn't matter. Control or none, he was still a man who needed to kill in order to live. Perhaps the only question that mattered was how long he would be able to postpone the inevitable.

Control or not, Garrick would never be a normal man again.

CHAPTER
TWENTY-THREE

Sunathri held his hand until they reached the chamber where he expected to find the other god-touched mages. The room was empty. He let his dark powers search out the mages, but found nothing.

His hunger raged, and Garrick turned to her.

Suni's eyes widened and she backed away.

"I thought you loved me," she whimpered as Garrick drew near.

"I do."

He grasped her arms and kissed her savagely, breathing her in, her scent sweet, her lips delicate, their contact savory as he absorbed her energy through every pore of his body until Sunathri fell lifeless to the floor.

He gasped and stared at her lying against the hard stone.

What had he done?

The crunch of a footstep came from behind.

Garrick whirled.

Two mages strode forward, fire blazing in their hands.

Garrick woke with a start. He was in his tent. It was still the middle of the night, dark, and quiet. The pure blackness of his hunger swirled within him, feeding off his dream like a buzzard on carrion.

A light footstep came from outside, twin to the one that first brought him awake. The fabric of his tent rustled. Someone working the ties.

A shadow lined the tent wall. A sharp burst of adrenaline spiked his veins and his hunger became rough against the back of his throat. He rose unsteadily from the cot and peered into the darkness.

Could Sunathri be returning?

Darien?

The figure finished untying the flaps.

A soft whisper came through the night, then the faint, but unmistakable odor of blood-laced Koradictine magic.

Garrick's throat tightened.

The assassin entered his tent, and Garrick reached for his link to the plane of magic. The flow of magestuff was tepid, and he had no inner force left to bring it with any greater speed. He whispered a word of sorcery and concentrated as hard as he possibly could.

The Koradictine's arm rose with the dull flash of a dagger.

He grunted and cast a simple spell of power that caught the mage across the shoulder just as he stabbed. The blade scored Garrick's ribs with acidic pain but did not make a serious wound.

Garrick's hunger struck like a snake.

The Koradictine gave a stifled scream as Garrick devoured his life force in one glorious breath. The mage's eyes reflected purple magelight as he faded. More footsteps fell heavy outside, running away.

Garrick rose from his cot, already feeling the strength of fresh life force roiling inside him. His blood pounded as he stepped to the tent's opening.

It was another Koradictine running away through the brush.

The Dorfort guard was rousing, but Garrick didn't wait for them. He chased the mage into the woods, contorting his hand and marshaling his new life force to blast energy into the brush. The mage crashed through the thicket, racing for his life and casting magic wildly behind him.

Garrick's pace brought him even, and he grabbed the Koradictine by the shoulder so that they tumbled over the grassy ground. Garrick rolled over him, digging his fingertips into the man's flesh and feasting on his energy in a surge of power that made him shudder. When it was done, Garrick stood, panting, and looked down at the dark husk that was all that remained of the mage.

Footsteps came from behind him.

"Lord Garrick?" a guard called.

"Stay back," he barked.

The guard stayed where he was, but another joined.

He felt Sunathri come forward, then Darien. He wanted to reach out to them. The hunger inside had been loosed, and it tasted their life force. He wanted to feast, but he held himself back

Perhaps Sunathri was right about him learning to control Braxidane's magic.

"Garrick?" Darien called.

"Are you all right?" Sunathri added as she came closer.

Darien stopped her, though, and they all waited there to see what Garrick would do.

Full control came slowly, but once he had a sense of stability about himself he collected himself and came out of the darkness.

"What happened?" Sunathri said.

"Koradictine scouts broke into camp," Garrick explained.

"I'm sorry," Darien said. "I'll speak to our sentries." But the glance he shared with Sunathri gave him away.

"This was no accident, was it?" Garrick said.

"What do you mean?"

Garrick's vision was sharp now despite the darkness. He saw how Darien's eyes grew hooded, and he felt the truth to his accusation. "You left this weakness open in hopes the orders would exploit it."

"I don't know what you're talking about."

"You fed me these spies like you would feed hamsters to a snake."

"I can't believe you would accuse me of putting you at risk that way," Darien said.

Garrick stared at his friend, feeling the nighttime expand around him. He understood what was happening. Neither Darien nor Sunathri could be found to have given such orders, or the armies around them would revolt. And, yet, the truth of their action was as clear to him as the two heaps of dead Koradictine mages he had created.

He breathed in the air of the woods.

Regardless of how he felt about his friends, he could not deny that he felt stronger than he had for weeks. He was ready to climb the mountain.

"It's been a long trip," he finally said. "Be light on your sentries if you find they were doing their best."

Then Garrick returned to his tent to prepare.

TWENTY-FOUR

Garrick sat on the cold face of a hard rock and watched the horizon turn a lighter shade.

He would not win today.

He had known it for some time, but couldn't voice it. It had been a grand plan, coming here to face the orders' god-touched mages, but now that they were here and the confrontation was coming, he realized certain truths. And one of those truths was that he would not win today.

How could he?

The orders' god-touched sorcerers were experienced, with wizardry greater than his. Ellesadil and Commander J'ravi had said that constantly, and despite Garrick's assurances that he would deal with that, they were both right. So he would lose. He would face these god-touched mages, and he would come out on the back end.

An owl beat its wings against the last of the night as it bore down upon unsuspecting prey. The air was damp against his skin, and the nocturnal calls of insects made the final strains of their evening music—music he had come to appreciate more with time. Around him, Dorfort's army and the last remnants of the Torean Freeborn prepared themselves for battle.

Garrick looked up at God's Tower.

The peak drew its name from one of the most ancient legends told at inns and taverns—the story of Abridar and Katha, two gods who held a great battle there. What would it have been like to see that? He wondered if Abridar and Katha were planewalkers. Did they still live? How long does a planewalker survive, after all? He thought about Braxidane. How many people had he used before Garrick? How many would come after?

He should have done something more to prepare.

Alistair would have—he would have worked to learn more about this place rather than waste time playing games with life force as Garrick had done. Then, again, Alistair did not suffer the same tax that Garrick did, so who could say what Alistair would have done?

It was too late now, anyway.

What was done was done. The Koradictine army lay in wait to the northeast, and the Lectodinian army was camped to the west. Today they would act in concert to pinch the Freeborn between them.

The Torean camp stirred with nervous energy as dawn approached. Some of them would die today, and they prepared themselves with professional diligence because it helped them avoid thinking about this fact. Warriors sharpened their weapons and tested their shields. Mages took their stations. Occasionally, though, they would glance toward Garrick's tent with expressions of anxiety and hope—the men and women of the Torean army looked to Darien and Sunathri to make decisions on the ground, but they looked to Garrick to win the day.

It struck him that the need to be led was natural—the need to feel communion with something bigger than yourself, to believe in something so strongly you could let go of what you couldn't handle and focus on only those things you could. He hadn't truly understood this until now. Those glances said that if each of them did their jobs, Garrick would defeat the god-touched mages and the day would be won. But if leadership required men who wanted to be led, it also needed a leader with vision and competence—things Garrick did not possess.

Garrick understood he was the only piece on the board that could stand between the orders and their domination of the plane, but he knew nothing of how to lead men beyond the fact that power corrupts.

Power bends the people who use it.

It was the main learning of his life.

This army stood testimony to the fact that Garrick himself had become a man who used others. They were here for one reason, after all. Take everything else away, and Garrick knew they were here because he had decided to confront the orders.

What price would these warriors and mages pay for his hubris?

How bad would it be?

All he could say for certain was that today he would meet two god-touched mages.

And, today, he could not win.

Darien emerged from his tent and swaggered toward Garrick. The plume at the top of his polished helm blazed in the morning sun. His armor plates gleamed silver.

"You've come a ways from Caledena," Garrick said.

"You're one to speak."

They each grinned.

"We may both be dead before this day is over," Garrick said.

"Perhaps," Darien replied. "But I doubt it."

"You are a true optimist, my friend."

"Guilty. But I have my reasons. Suni's mages are rested and our forces are in place. The field scouts suggest that our hidden mages remain undiscovered. My warriors are prepared. And you, Garrick, are rested. We couldn't ask for more."

"It is still not enough," Garrick replied. He looked at his friend and gave him his confession. "I have no real plan for my part."

Darien gave him a sly grin.

"I've seen your work. I have no fears."

Garrick raised a doubting eyebrow. "Then perhaps you should be the one to climb the mountain."

"If all else fails," Darien said, "put everything on griffin five."

Garrick laughed, then pursed his lips. "Your father would be proud of you today," he said in a low voice.

"One step at a time, Garrick. One step at a time. Speaking of which, it's time I go check on preparations. Fight well, my friend. I'll see you this evening."

"Aye. Fight well, Darien."

He watched as Darien walked among Dorfort's warriors. His friend spoke quietly with each. He listened to stories about their weapons and eased their fears.

Suni, too, spent time among the Freeborn.

Garrick found himself oddly jealous of them both, but he knew he couldn't find it within himself to do what they did. Theirs was a true form of leadership, something he did not have.

Soldiers looked at him with questions in their eyes.

He went to a kettle and spooned soup into a bowl. He didn't need to eat, but the act seemed important. The heat of the bowl on his hand made him feel normal. The feel of the spoon felt natural.

Suddenly, footsteps crashed from the brush behind him.

Garrick whirled to see a man emerge from a copse of trees. Recognition dawned as he was reaching for his link to the plane of magic. It was the ranger who had saved him in the alleys of Dorfort. The man stood a head taller than Garrick. The muscles on his arms flexed as he hefted a battle ax. His beard was still bristly, and his bald pate reflected the sun.

"What are *you* doing here?" Garrick said.

"Wouldn't miss this for the world," the man said.

Garrick shook his head with wonder. "I am glad you came. Fight well."

"You also," the ranger replied.

And at that moment, a buzz crossed the field. Horns blew, and warriors grabbed their weapons.

"Positions!" Darien called, riding forward.

Suni raced to Garrick. She gripped his upper arm and rose to her toes to let her lips brush his cheek. "Fight well, Garrick," she said. "Go with good fortune."

Then she rushed to her mages.

Garrick's hand rose to his cheek as he watched her leave. The sensation of her lips tingled for a long moment. Then he snapped out of it and looped his belt around his waist, settled both a dagger and a short sword into their places, and mounted his horse.

He glanced up the mountain, then spurred the horse to race into the pass that climbed toward the chamber at the peak of God's Tower.

He was well into the foothills before he realized that, once again, he had forgotten to ask the ranger's name.

TWENTY-FIVE

The horse kicked up a billowing cloud of dust as Garrick thundered through the lowlands and entered a sheer pass that twisted farther upward. Wind whistled, and his shirt whipped against his chest. The terrain grew rockier until he came to a place no beast could carry him, so he left the horse free to roam. The animal was trained well and should remain close by. Not that he expected to need it.

Garrick climbed the steep path by hand and foot, picking his way upward as quickly as he could until he arrived at a dark crevasse that opened into the heart of the mountain. A glance downward gave him a perfect view of the massive armies of the orders gathered to the east and west, their Koradictine and Lectodinian mages wearing colorful robes of red and blue.

Distracted, he stepped blindly into the crevasse and recoiled as a stinging jolt showered him with red sparks.

He scuttled backward and felt magic covering the entrance.

He approached again, touching his link and letting magestuff flow through his gates. He splayed his hand, whispered magic, and channeled energy. This was a warding spell, so he poured magestuff into the barrier and spoke a word of power Alistair had once taught him that worked on locks. The barrier shattered, and he slipped through the opening with renewed confidence.

The passage inside was cold and rose so steeply that he sometimes needed to use both hands to climb onward.

He cast magelight upon the edge of his dagger, gripping it with nervous energy.

The passage necked down, forcing him to squeeze through rocky gaps that were cold and hard. Soon he came to a chamber the size of Alistair's laboratory. There was power here. He felt it as an unpleasant tingle inside his belly.

A caustic wall of odor hit him like a mix of vinegar and rotten seaweed.

An amorphous mass of green and brown slime coalesced before him, a strange, formless thing with appendages that might have been eyes. Bile caught in his throat as the creature sluiced a tentacle toward him.

Garrick slashed with his dagger.

He missed, but it bought him time to draw his sword and hack at it. The slime fell back with a hiss, but his blade became warped and useless. He tossed it aside, giving the creature time to reach another slimy arm toward him. He ducked and funneled magestuff into his spell work.

Fire sprang from his palm, and a roaring sizzle filled the chamber with noxious mist.

Garrick's head swam, and the chamber spun. He fell to one knee and found the air cleaner near the floor. So he drew a quick breath, pulled his bandana over his mouth, and rolled away as the creature swung a mottled arm the size of a tree trunk.

From this angle, Garrick saw he had burned a gaping hole into the creature, but the wound didn't stop it. It swung another gooey pod, forcing him to cast a barrier that deflected the blow before unleashing another stream of fire. A roar like water hitting oil filled Garrick's ears. Swamp fog brought tears to his eyes.

He covered his face and ran through the mist, preparing himself to crash into the girth of the creature's bulk.

Instead, his leap found nothing but air.

He tumbled headlong through the chamber, rolling by luck into another small crease that fell into another tunnel, slanting upward. The creature didn't follow. Had Garrick killed it? Now was not the time to find out.

He scrambled away, crawling on hands and feet and elbows and knees until he was certain he was out of danger.

Then he sat back against ice-cold rock and gasped for breath.

That had been close. So close. After all this, his story had nearly come to its anonymous end at the hands of a magical ward-beast. "That would be fitting, eh?" he said to himself.

What dangers were the Koradictine and Lectodinian god-touched mages finding?

He stood up and waved the magelight of his dagger before him.

This tunnel curved in a lazy spiral further upward. He climbed until he came to a place where the passage suddenly opened to a platform like a stairwell might open to a roof, and where brilliant light blinded him.

He blinked and shaded his eyes from the blazing light with one hand.

It was as if the room had been sliced cleanly from the mountain, leaving the peak floating in open air above. The floor was smooth and polished, as was the ceiling above. They both reflected the sunlight that streamed through the non-existent walls as natural as day.

This, Garrick realized, was the chamber atop God's Tower.

CHAPTER
TWENTY-SIX

"Looks like it should crush us, doesn't it?"

Garrick whirled to find a man standing behind him. He wore a blue shirt with white laces running up the front, tanned breeches that clung to him like a second skin, and gemstones that glittered from his fingers. His dark hair was cut short along the top and sides but flowed in a cascading river down his back. His cheeks were sunken. Dark circles ringed his eyes.

"And you would be?" Garrick said.

"Parathay," the Lectodinian said with oily smoothness. "Commander, lover of books, and occasional mage. At your service."

The Lectodinian bowed with a flourish, then gave a cold grin.

"Marvelous place for a battle, isn't it?"

The Lectodinian's spell came so quickly Garrick barely had time to cast a barrier. When it came, the shield was weak, but enough. The Lectodinian's magic was cold as ice, bold, and strong. It was also exploratory, an early volley meant merely to test him.

Garrick glared and struck a defensive pose. He brought life force up to support his shield as Parathay strolled about him with a confident swagger.

"You thought I would wait for Jormar?"

"It seems only appropriate."

"Koradictines are always late. It will be their eventual downfall, you know? They have no discipline, no vision."

"And what, I wonder," Garrick said, "would a Koradictine say about the Lectodinians?"

A throaty voice came from behind Garrick.

"He would say they have no creativity."

Garrick instinctively rolled to the side and came to one knee as a bloody flash of fire blasted by him.

"Greetings, Jormar el'Mor," Parathay said. "So good to see you."

The Koradictine was a large man, fleshed out as if he rarely left an empty dinner table. His bulging red robe flowed around him like a skirt. A yellow sash rode up over his ample gut.

They glowered at each other.

These were the most powerful mages on the Adruic plane, and it was obvious they could barely stand to be in the same room together.

"Best friends, I see."

"Common goals make great partnerships," Parathay said as he cast another bolt of cold energy at Garrick.

Garrick's shield throbbed, and his hands grew numb. "And when those goals are no longer common?" he said.

"We'll address that when it becomes necessary," Jormar responded.

The Koradictine spoke thunderous words. Lightning flashed, and Garrick tumbled once again to avoid a shower of sparks redolent with the odors of burnt honey and curdled blood. Where Parathay's magic was cold and hollow, Jormar's carried overwhelming heat and vitality. Sweat beaded on Garrick's brow. He retreated to give himself space, totally on the defensive now. His life force dwindled, and the other mages seemed to be just now warming to their work. He needed a moment, so he latched onto his link and cast flames at Parathay.

The Lectodinian caught the spell with one hand, then kneaded its energy like clay between his palms until it was a ball of brilliant blue light that he eventually absorbed, the energy simply seeping into his skin until it was gone.

Parathay grinned at Garrick. "Quite tasty," he said. His eyes flickered with life. "Is this the best a Torean can manage?"

The Lectodinian twisted his hands together and a cold web whipped itself around Garrick, its filaments burning against his skin. His life force was drawn toward it like iron to a magnet. Rather than fight it, sent life force through his arms and legs to use the net's momentum against itself. The attack bent away and simply burned itself into a cloud of gray ash.

"Fine shot, Parathay," Jormar el'Mor said. "Alas, it didn't do the job."

The Koradictine's body jiggled as he whipped his arm forward to throw a wave of power toward Garrick. A flow of golden current rolled through the cavern with dark fishes riding its breaking crest, their oversized jaws clacking with metallic teeth.

The wave pushed him backward with a rush of salt and sewage.

The fish bit into his legs and arms.

Garrick set gates and cast what remained of his life force at the fish. They fell away, leaving him gasping for breath and in smoldering pain, prone on the floor, and sopping wet as the wave died out.

He was near the edge of the chamber now, nearly blinded by sunlight, but able to make out the ground below. The Lectodinian army had closed in on the western flank, and the Koradictines were pinching from the east. The Torean decoy mages bought them time, but the eventual outcome was obvious. The orders' armies were too large. The Toreans' would soon be destroyed.

His muscles ached and his vision swam.

His life force was all but gone, and the god-touched mages of the Lectodinian and Koradictine orders strode forward, each vibrant and each with wickedness pasted on their faces.

It was over, he realized.

He would not win.

Despite its inevitability, the thought made him angry. He had been a pawn his whole life. If he was going to die today, he was not going to go out as a meek apprentice.

Garrick grimaced against his pain, willed himself to one knee, then stood as straight and as tall as he could.

He turned then. Resigned. Turned and faced the Koradictine and Lectodinian god-touched mages one last time.

TWENTY-SEVEN

Smoke and swordsong rolled over the battlefield as Darien rode among his soldiers. Blood colored the soil, and the screams of the wounded filled the air. Dorfort's army had held their own until a gathering of Koradictines cast great bolts of magic across their positions.

He called for a retreat to the next line, but three of his men were trapped.

Darien spurred his horse forward, hacking at Koradictine mercenaries as he raced across the field. A battle-ax clanged against his armor and a sword slashed at his thigh, but his men slipped through the opening he created and they raced away with shouts of victory.

Koradictine troops chased until a line of Freeborn mages leapt upon the fortified ridge and cast magic into the fray. Flames of blue and orange gave Darien the time he needed, and the hooves of his horse thundered as he made the Torean line.

An arrow pierced the chest of one black-garbed mage, though, and she fell screaming.

Darien's men turned to defend once again.

The retreat had been successful, but Darien understood the critical word in that thought was "retreat."

The orders were winning. They had more men, and their wizards were stronger. It was only a matter of time. The end was drawing near, and there was nothing he could do for it.

His gaze went to the peak above.

CHAPTER
TWENTY-EIGHT

Sweat poured down Garrick's face, and his body ached. His life force was spent and his hunger ravaged his mind. He had used his rage to force himself to his feet, but once there, facing the order's god-touched, he had nothing left.

Braxidane! he thought, or maybe he spoke the name aloud, he couldn't tell.

Braxidane!

Help me!

There was no answer.

He could barely stay on his feet.

"You were unwise to call us out, apprentice," Jormar said.

"Now you'll pay the price," Parathay finished.

Hunger stirred deep inside Garrick, seeming to rise to the movement of the other two. He felt the god-touched mages as they prepared their killing blows. The portly Koradictine soul was a blazing kiln of fire, and the Lectodinian's the cold breath of winter. Their dichotomy was as painful as a blade.

A thought came with crystalline purity.

He remembered his conversation with Suni, and his eyes widened.

"The most complex spells require the least energy," she had said, "but the greatest clarity of thought."

He hoped this was true.

Jormar raised a hand, and Parathay's eyes focused into intense beams.

Garrick put his thoughts together, setting about creating a spell armed only with a vision of how it ought to flow—matching order with chaos, setting gates and creating an empty loop, a vessel he knit together but left vacant of either magestuff or life force.

He timed his sorcerous phrasing just as Jormar and Parathay unleashed their red and blue streaks of magic.

Garrick pulled on the beast inside him, opening its vampiric hunger to the avalanche of Jormar's power and pouring it into Parathay's draw.

It was like catching a smithy's hammer with his lungs.

He gasped and twisted his mind into a loop, folding his hunger back upon itself and tying it into a knot. Numbness crawled up his arm. Electricity crackled. Jormar's heat mixed with Parathay's chill, and as Garrick pulled the loop tight, the two veins of magic twined around themselves to create a pulsing thread of violet energy that writhed across the chamber and wrapped itself around him, constricting tighter with each breath.

Garrick ignored the pain. Ignored the pressure. He forced the ends of the stream together, Koradictine to Lectodinian, Lectodinian to Koradictine.

Time stretched.

Light flared.

He thought he heard the orders' mages scream.

And in that moment, nothing existed.

No Darien, no Suni, no Arianna.

No slaves in Arderveer or villagers in Sjesko.

No God's Tower.

No Caledena, no Baron Fahid, no Alistair.

In that moment, there was nothing in this world but Garrick and his sense of balance.

Action and consequence, he thought.

Consequence and action.

When the cacophony finally died it was like light being doused, leaving behind only a low drone of power and the rasp of Garrick's breathing.

Slowly, painfully, he raised his gaze.

The orders' mages were frozen in place, Parathay casting his draining thread and Jormar throwing his bolt of power, but now the two threads looped through Garrick's device—they were entangled, frozen, their faces fixed with grimaces and their eyes open in shock. Their sorcery was locked in a recursive loop, Parathay endlessly being fed and Jormar constantly drained.

Garrick lay there, feeling like a scarecrow on fire, his bones feeling detached and his body loose enough that he could swivel at every joint.

He had done it. He had survived.

He had nothing left to give.

But he had won.

TWENTY-NINE

Garrick crawled to the edge of the chamber and peered at the battlefield below. The orders appeared to have the upper hand, though it was difficult to see.

His hunger surged at the sensation of bloodshed. His stomach churned for it even at this distance. He forced himself to stand, raising himself with the cautious, ginger movements of a newborn foal though the effort nearly made him pass out.

The battle raged below.

It moved something in him.

He reached his hand out to what might have been the wall but found passage through was possible. So he stepped directly from the chamber to the surface of the mountain and found himself standing suddenly calf-deep in snow so suddenly he nearly fell over.

The bitter cold of altitude bit his lungs.

He shivered.

He turned to look back into the chamber but saw nothing beyond the snow and barren rock that ran with mineraled veins. His horse stood a few hundred yards down the mountainside, so he staggered toward it. Darien and Sunathri needed him. The Freeborn needed him. The battle raging below, the power of life force. It all needed him.

His vision fogged as he took a step toward the animal, then another and another before falling over. He crawled, shivering so hard his teeth rattled.

"Horse," he yelled into the wind.

The beast looked up.

"Come here!"

He stood one more time. Miraculously, the animal came his way. He pulled himself over its back. His body was drained and his muscles ached, but he clutched the animal's mane well enough for the horse to carry him, and as they moved he got a leg over.

A moment later he was racing down the mountainside.

CHAPTER

THIRTY

At the southern pass, four Lectodinian mages attacked the Freeborn's flank, their light blue tunics whipping in the wind as they bore down.

Sunathri called three wizards to follow her, and set off to stop them.

The southern pass was critical.

The Freeborn had arranged most of their forces to the east and west, hoping that the surprise of Torean mages at the orders' rear guard would reduce their southern offensives. The gambit had succeeded for a time, but the orders had regrouped and were beginning to expose their weakest areas.

She had to stop them here.

Sunathri touched her link and waited for energy to pool. She was tired, and her casting took more time than she liked. Green and red flares burst from her palms, taking two of the men. The third continued to ride away.

"Come on!" she yelled.

She and her Freeborn chased the remaining Lectodinian through a row of sycamore trees.

It was a trap, though.

She brought her horse up as soon as she recognized it, but it was too late.

A row of warriors rose before them, shouting battle cries, their swords and halberds flashing in the sun as they raced forward. A handful of mages cast spells from positions behind the warriors.

"Retreat!" she called.

Her men brandished their weapons and spread out to perform a controlled maneuver.

She cast a shield just in time to deflect sorcery, but green sparks flew around her and numbness buzzed her arm. These spell casters were fresh, their magic was strong.

Swords clanged on shields.

A man screamed.

Three mercenaries closed in on one of her men, and Sunathri cast a bolt to save him.

The Lectodinians took advantage of the distraction.

A bolt of energy struck her mount full in the chest. Sunathri rolled off the animal as it fell. She scrambled to her feet and cast a wild fan of flames to protect herself.

One of her men was pierced through by a spear.

Another was dismounted.

The orders' mercenaries swept around the two men, but they fought on, crying out Sunathri's name and giving her time to cast another spell.

She stepped onto a rock, leaving herself exposed for an instant but also providing a broader range of vision. She gathered as much energy as she could summon and worked to set a simple series of gates. Her spellwork wasn't as sharp as she wanted, but this magic was basic and she needed to save her men. Flames spewed from her hands to pour down upon the southern flank.

Men died.

She fell to one knee as her energy waned, flames still flowing.

Below her, the Lectodinian's lips twisted.

Sunathri turned her aim to engulf the mage, but she moved too slowly. The Lectodinian raised one arm, and a flash flared from his palm. Fingers of purple lightning clutched at the sky, and everything froze in the electric strobe—men with gleaming swords raised, tree limbs bent with the wind, the grimace on the face of the Lectodinian mage as his robe caught fire, and Sunathri, leader of the Freeborn, standing alone and exposed atop the mountain rock, an expression of defiance etched on her face.

THIRTY-ONE

As the horse raced down the snowy mountaintop, past the tree line, and over the rocky trail that led down the mountain, Garrick held onto the horse's neck as if it were the only thing left in the world.

His legs quivered, and his arms burned. His bloated eyes blurred as he burst onto the battlefield behind the Koradictine line.

His hunger was a beast of its own.

That beast was the force by which he moved. It was the presence that filled his mind. And, unfettered by the balance of life force, this beast that was Braxidane's dark magic was on the hunt. It found steel ringing against steel, warriors screaming with pain. It found horses braying, a field that erupted with sorcerous flashes, and a pallor of life force that hung over that field like an unearthly blanket of power.

The presence of every soldier on the battlefield was as pure and clear as if each was a point on a map.

Garrick—that small part of him that was still human—felt it all, sensed every movement, every slice of a blade, every fiery spell as it burned through a battle line. His hunger, starved and angry, inhaled voracious gulps of energy that fed his body, its essence so exquisite and so intoxicating he nearly fell. He pulled his dagger and leapt into the scrum. Three warriors died in silent surprise, and his hunger fed. A Lectodinian wizard whirled, fingers splayed for the attack, but Garrick ripped his life force from him with nearly effortless haste.

Steel sliced into his leg.

He destroyed the wielder as rapidly as the cut healed itself. Horrified cries rang across the battlefield as he tore souls from men.

The Freeborn army cried in victory.

"Lord Garrick!"

"God-touched!"

As they called his name, the Freeborn fell back, leaving space for Garrick but blocking their opponent's escape to create a killing field for him that he did not resist.

Black hunger crackled over his fingertips as he pulled more and more life force. Mages crumbled. Mercenary soldiers ran. Still Garrick gorged on the energy here. He funneled it into his sorcery to bring death until, finally, the Koradictine lines broke completely and their mages fled at full run.

A few of Dorfort's guard gave chase, but most turned west to throw their lot to those fighting the Lectodinian army.

Garrick, too, ran toward the Lectodinian line, racing against time, realizing this hunger would fade, unwilling to give up this momentum. He felt his hunger fade, though. Despite his efforts, his rage calmed.

The plumes of Darien's helm rose over the battlefield, and Garrick's heart soared.

Then he saw them.

The wounded and the dead.

Men and women scattered across the grounds, twisted and disfigured, crying, and groaning. They lay with limbs hacked away, and with bleeding wounds and faces streaked with dirt and sweat.

And his life force pulled at him, stronger than he had ever felt it pull. He tried to concentrate on the Lectodinian threat, but just as the hunger swelled in a bursting wave that could not be denied.

Braxidane's sweet voice came then.

You have taken …

"No!" he called.

… now you must give.

He came to a Torean wizard with a gaping hole in his chest and dark blood pooling on the dirt below him.

Garrick poured life force into the wounds, twining the gash together and knitting the bone of his leg. Moments later, the man breathed easier.

"Praise you, Lord Garrick," the man said.

The next mage was dead beyond retrieval.

A warrior with a cracked skull had bare life remaining, but bare life was still life, so Garrick repaired the damage and left him sleeping.

A man had been felled by an arrow through the heart—irretrievable.

The next had lost his leg and lay on the ground sobbing and bleeding and muttering incoherently. Garrick stanched the wound and comforted the man.

"You'll see your grandsons grow now, sir."

Then he left to find the next wounded.

And so it went.

Case after case, after case after case, Garrick raced through the Torean ranks, mending damage, repairing limbs, and saving lives.

And once they were healed, the warriors ran toward the Lectodinian line like frenzied dervishes, shouting "Lord Garrick!" as if the mere mention of his name would destroy their enemy.

The Lectodinian army fell back.

Still Garrick found wounded warriors.

A female mage lay in shock, her leg nearly severed.

Garrick funneled life force into her, tying vessels together, knitting muscles, connecting bone and marrow. In the process, he found something else there, too—a beating heart, another life force, powerful and strong. He smiled and considered telling her of the child, then decided against it.

He turned to the next man in line.

It was the ranger from the alley. Sweat rolled off the man's bald pate. His bristled, spittle-knotted beard quivered with his pain as he looked at Garrick. A deep gash scored his side.

Garrick funneled life force into the man.

Despite his pain, the man was strong inside. Garrick felt balance to his purpose, the power of his conviction. Emotion boiled up inside Garrick then, an emotion that had nothing to do with magic or planewalkers or his internal life forces.

When Garrick was done, tears ran down his face.

"What is your name?" he asked.

"What?" the ranger said.

"I asked you your name."

"Fredric," the big man said. "My name is Fredric."

Garrick smiled.

"Rest now, Fredric. You have done well."

A cheer rang over the battlefield.

Voices of soldiers of Dorfort rose in a vast cry.

"Darien! Darien! Darien!" they yelled.

The Lectodinians were routed.

The battle of God's Tower was over.

THIRTY-TWO

Darien rode toward Garrick, his face sweat-drenched and his armor spattered with mud. A trickle of blood ran down his arm, and his leg was stained crimson. He raised his father's sword over his head and shouted above the voices of his men.

"Hail, Garrick!" he cried to his warriors.

The army cheered, rattling their swords and beating their shields. Mages shouted Garrick's name. Darien's smile was bright, and his eyes beamed in the late afternoon sun.

Garrick stood.

His life force was nearly balanced. His hunger was not raging, nor did he feel the deep whispers of excess. He was tired, but it was a good tired. If he could just stay this way forever, he thought. But while the rest of the Torean army could cheer, Garrick knew that was not going to happen.

He scanned the field for Sunathri but did not find her. He glanced at Darien, his chest growing tighter and his eyes wide with the question.

"Where is Sunathri?" Garrick asked.

A dark cloud crossed Darien's face. The cheers fell to silence.

"She was defending the south pass last I saw," Darien replied.

Garrick pushed through the gathering and sprinted toward the pass.

Darien rode, his horse easily outracing Garrick.

Still Garrick ran, his stride a graceful lope and his arms and legs pumping. He vaulted broken pikes and destroyed supply wagons, sprinting like a deer through brambles, his straw-colored hair blazed in the late sun.

More men on horseback raced past him.

Garrick reached the saddle of the next horse that came by and, in mid-stride, hefted himself up behind the man. The rider spurred his animal and they rejoined the chase. When they caught the group, Darien had already dismounted.

Four men stood around him as he knelt.

Garrick slid from the horse before it came to a rest.

Sunathri lay on the ground with three other Toreans. Blood pooled under her, and her rib cage had been ripped with a great gash. An entire detail of Lectodinian mercenaries and sorcerers lay dead around them.

An eerie separation came over him.

He did not hear, did not smell. It was as if this wasn't real, as if he was viewing it from afar. Except that he *was* there. This *was* happening.

Garrick ran to Sunathri's side, brushing Darien out of the way.

He put his hand to her forehead and felt for her life force.

There was nothing.

Nothing.

He opened one of her lids. Her eyes were dull and lifeless.

A tear trailed like fire down his cheek.

Sunathri's body lay before him like an empty shell waiting to receive the life force he could give her. He could do it. He could bring her back, but then she would be fueled by magic and her eyes would carry the cold light that Alistair's did. For a brief moment, he actually considered it. But then he remembered the shrill sound of pain in his superior's call as the mage stood alone in his desolate manor yard, and he remembered Braxidane's contempt for him as his simple desire to save life served to destroy it instead.

It was suddenly very hard to breathe.

"Braxidane!"

Garrick yelled as he leapt atop the same rock where Sunathri had made her final defense.

"Braxidane!"

The wind whistled through the clearing.

Sweat from his brow dripped onto the rock.

Perhaps the mages around him would think him daft as he was speaking aloud, but he didn't care.

"It's not fair," he yelled into the wind in a raw voice. "It's not fair."

For a moment Garrick thought he heard his superior's voice. *There is no 'fair,' Garrick*, he thought he heard. But he was wrong. Garrick may well be as insane as the Freeborn would think he was, but he wasn't going to delude himself on purpose. He was on his own now. Braxidane wasn't with him as he fought the order's god-touched mages inside God's Tower, and he wasn't going to be here on the battlefield.

He despised the planewalker then.

He despised Braxidane for his power and for his callous nature. He hated him for the way Braxidane played with his psyche, hated him for this "gift" of balance that gave him the blood-mad exhilaration of ripping souls in battle in tandem with the heartbreaking joy of bringing life to the wounded.

"What is it you want, Braxidane?" he finally whispered. "Why are you doing this?"

He was met with only silence.

Garrick turned his bloodshot gaze to the battlefield.

The mages stared at him with expectant eyes. Sunathri was dead

—the news spread quickly. Now the mages of her order looked to him.

He was god-touched. He was the one who had changed their fortunes, the one who had brought them back from the very edge of death itself. He felt numb. Bile burned in his stomach.

You monster, Garrick thought. *You had this in mind since the first moment.*

He sensed Sunathri's life force in the clearing around him, just as he had once tasted Arianna's life force. He felt her flow through him, warming him. He tasted her memories, so solid that he thought for a moment she might have risen from the dead.

And he remembered her kiss, her willingness to give herself up for her cause, the fire that had been in her eyes the first time he saw her.

Then she was gone.

THIRTY-THREE

Garrick retreated up the mountain to be alone, but instead of solace, he found that the high perch merely served to give him a better view from which to watch the army as it dealt with the blood price of this victory. He watched as columns of black smoke disappeared into thin air, and he watched as others buried their dead in the same pits and trenches that, earlier in the week, they had dug as defenses. He watched as mages picked through the battlefield to retrieve mementos and other reminders of the dead so that they might be delivered back to their families, and he watched smiths and tanners and others as they bent to repair whatever could be repaired for the trip home.

Yes, Garrick thought from this distant perch high on the mountainside, the price for this victory was quite clear.

And as the perch gave him his view, it also lent a view of those who remained of the Freeborn. They looked to him with pressure in their gazes—unspoken, but clear. Crushing. Stifling. That pressure wrapped its tentacles around Garrick like a serpent of the sea. It squeezed his breath away.

It was too much, all too much.

The reality of these movements.

The pressure of the Freeborn's expectation.

The certainty of his own future as a pawn to a planewalker. Braxidane's explanations came to him in full force now. Events were happening, and sitting alone he understood what Braxidane meant when he'd warned Garrick that those events were larger and more complex than he would ever understand.

He drew a breath of pure mountain air and saw a single truth, though.

He could not take Sunathri's place.

As he watched the men and women of Dorfort's army clean the field of battle, Garrick felt a gap greater than anyone else on that field possibly could.

He understood something no one else could possibly understand.

He had been angry at Braxidane because his superior had not come to his aid. It was a fair anger, he supposed. But as nighttime stole over the horizon and the air grew crisp, Garrick felt a deeper truth. Braxidane *would* have come if he could have—just as the other planewalkers who were so clearly behind the powers of Jormar and Parathay would have come to the aid of the orders' god-touched mages if *they* could have.

But all the planewalkers had stayed away.

All of them.

Garrick wished he had paid more attention to Braxidane when the planewalker described his connections but, then, Garrick had never really listened to anyone with power before. At best, he had taken only the pieces he wanted to hear and used them to support his own point of view. But seeing Afarat J'ravi work, then Suni, and then Darien had changed that—or had at least rattled that practice hard enough that he was seeing things differently.

This battle was not done.

Braxidane said pacts existed among the planewalkers, and they each paid prices for meddling in places like Adruin. Garrick may not understand the depths of planewalker politics, but the fact that neither Braxidane nor the others had come meant there was something deeper here—something bigger, something that could well entail the whole of Existence as the planewalkers knew it.

He knew Braxidane would not have been happy to lose him, so it wasn't hard to guess that the planewalkers who lost Parathay and Jormar el'Mor would not be happy, either. If he understood power as well as he thought he did, those planewalkers would not stand such a defeat for long, nor would the orders themselves.

It all added up to say that the price paid on this battlefield, great though it was, was just one installment of what might well be many, many more.

EPILOGUE

It was evening time when Garrick returned from the mountain. The grounds had been tended, the dead buried or burned. Those still wounded had been made ready to travel. Garrick came to the camp having decided his future would entail traveling on his own. He could not stay in the city. He knew better than to think the orders would stop hunting him, and anywhere he went would become a target. No one around him would be safe. So he would see the army back to their home, but then he would set out to face the orders on his own.

As for Braxidane and the rest of the planewalkers, well ... what could he do?

He was just a man. He would deal with those issues in whatever manner he could, and leave the rest for those who could handle them.

He was ready for this, though.

He would remember.

Braxidane had once said there was no fairness in this world, no justice. But Garrick knew better. He would see to it that the orders paid for what they had done to Alistair, and Arianna, and Sunathri.

The prey would finally become the predator.

As for what Braxidane would pay, he didn't know.

But justice *did* exist.

It existed because he said it did.

This life he was choosing would allow him to deal with the orders in quieter ways, and in fashions he couldn't manage if he were in a group such as the Freeborn. The idea of being on his own—of being a vigilante, of sorts—had been of great comfort sitting on the mountain, as it settled over him, and now, as he made his way toward Darien's tent, it felt even more solid.

He arrived there to find his friend engaged in heated discussions with Reynard, a gawky mage who was well-liked among the Freeborn. Mages and members of the guard were gathered around them.

"I don't care what you think," Darien said. "We're not going to start for home without the horses properly healthy. We need them curried and fed before the evening is out."

"Which we will accomplish through our magic," Reynard replied.

Garrick's appearance brought a hush to the field.

"Garrick," Darien said. "It's good to see you."

Garrick nodded. "What's wrong?"

"Lord Garrick," Reynard said. "The men are tired, and Commander J'ravi is commanding us to expend energy we do not need to give."

"The horses need to be curried by hand," Darien said. "There is more to this than cleanliness, and the horses know the difference."

Every gaze fell upon Garrick.

"The horses prefer to be curried by hand," he said. "And a wise traveler takes care of his animal."

Reynard gave a sigh that did nothing to hide his annoyance but turned to the Freeborn. "As Garrick says, we will curry the horses by hand."

"No," Garrick replied. "This is as *Commander J'ravi* said. He has earned that respect and more."

Reynard held Garrick's gaze a moment too long. "I agree, Lord

Garrick." He held his hand to Darien. "I apologize, Commander. I meant no disrespect."

Darien shook Reynard's hand.

"I will be in my tent, Commander J'ravi," Garrick said to Darien. "When you are finished with preparations, I would like a word." Then Garrick turned to leave.

"Lord Garrick?" Reynard said.

He hesitated.

"The order needs a leader if it is going to grow into Sunathri's vision. Will you serve?"

"I am a poor choice."

"You are god-touched."

"That alone makes me an unwise choice."

"With all due respect, Lord. You are the only one who thinks that."

The mages looked to Garrick again. Garrick said nothing. Life force stirred inside him, though, and he felt the urgency of Braxidane's desire. He knew better than to take command of the Freeborn. He had no desire to lead, and no skills. And he would not expose Sunathri's order to the whims of this abysmal force inside him.

"The Lectodinians remain strong," Reynard continued. "And we cannot be foolish enough to think the Koradictines will not rise from their ashes. We have to grow our roots now."

"I come with considerable baggage," Garrick said. "The order does not want me at its helm."

"Then we are lost," Reynard said.

The wizards murmured with disappointment.

"You are not lost."

All eyes turned to Darien.

"The only way the Freeborn would be lost would be to coerce Garrick into serving against his will. He must be free to decline, otherwise you corrupt the base ideal of Sunathri's vision for the Torean House itself."

"We need a leader," Reynard replied.

"If you would have me," Darien said, "I would lead your house."

Reynard smiled. "You are no mage."

"You're right. But I believe in what Sunathri stood for. I have fought for it. And I've grown up amid those who organize things. I can help you build this order."

The mages shared glances as Darien continued.

"But I am not blind to the fact that I cannot cast magic, and without that I might well struggle to lead. So, if the Torean Freeborn will have me I propose to name a board of mages to provide me counsel in this area. My first two selections will be you, Reynard, and, of course, Garrick."

"I'm not joining the Freeborn," Garrick said.

"You don't have to be Freeborn for me to ask your opinion. It's always best to hear all sides in a conflict. In fact, your voice, coming as a free citizen, brings its own value."

Garrick had nothing to say. He didn't want to tell Darien of his decision to set out on his own in this public moment.

"It could work," Reynard said, turning to look at Garrick. "Will you serve as Darien's counsel?"

Garrick put his hands on his hips.

He thought about Sunathri.

He remembered the velvet touch of her kiss and the strength of her passion.

Reynard was right. This arrangement could work. And he wanted to do something for Sunathri.

"I will be away often," he said. "And for long periods."

"Your learnings in these travels could aid the order," Darien replied, his question of what Garrick's words portended almost hidden by his tone.

"My god-touch makes me dangerous," Garrick replied

"And half of our army is alive due to that same touch."

Garrick nodded.

The proposed arrangement was really no different from the

arrangement they had come to God's Tower under, and Darien's response told him he was free to travel on his own as he planned.

"I can live with it," he said. "Or at least try."

"Then I will serve, too," Reynard replied.

The mages gave a disjointed cheer.

After a moment, Darien raised his hand and everything quieted.

"I have only one requirement for taking this position."

"Which is?" Reynard asked.

"The decision must be unanimous."

A smile grew over Reynard's lips, and he turned to the rest of the mages. "Are there any of the Torean House of the Freeborn who would reject Darien proposal?"

Faces turned to faces, all afraid of what might happen next.

No voice spoke against the arrangement.

"It is done, then," Reynard said. "Darien of Dorfort is the Torean Lord Superior."

The order cheered once again, and this time Darien did not stop them.

This is the end of *Rogue Mage*. I greatly value feedback. If you have enjoyed this story so far, please consider returning to your favorite booksellers and leaving a review.

The story of Garrick, Darien, and the struggle between the orders continues in *Champion Mage*, available as another tenth-anniversary edition of *Saga of the God-Touched Mage*.

The Saga of the God-Touched Mage
(10th Anniversary Edition)
includes

Apprentice Mage
Rogue Mage
Champion Mage
God Mage

Acknowledgments

The universe of Adruin and All of Existence has many people to thank for its existence, not the least of which are Tim Brown, Mike Cox, Ken and Jackie Peters, and my wife, Lisa.

I need to single out a few others for their efforts beyond all the rest.

My friend, collaborator, and pre-reader John Bodin's help was—as always—superlative. I want to thank my daughter, Brigid, for stepping into the fray when I needed her. My thanks also to Amy Sterling-Casil for her very generous commentary you can find at the front of this volume. And I want to give thanks to both my original cover artist, Rachel Carpenter, who was great fun to work with and who did a fantastic job bringing Garrick to life, and to Lisa Silverthorne who blew my mind with her great work on this 10th Anniversary edition.

Mostly, though, I have to thank Lisa for everything she's done for me. Saga of the God-Touched Mage has gone through more twists and turns than I could ever have predicted when the idea first hit, and she's been with me through every step. (Don't worry, honey. It's really done. Really, I mean it. It's done. You don't have to read it for the 111th time!).

About Ron Collins

Ron Collins is a bestselling Science Fiction and Dark Fantasy author who writes across the spectrum of speculative fiction.

Both his science fiction series, *Stealing the Sun*, and his fantasy series, *Saga of the God-Touched Mage*, have been bestsellers. His short fiction has received a Writers of the Future prize. He has published numerous short stories in venues such as *Analog, Asimov's, Pulphouse*, and the *Fiction River* original anthology project. His short stories have been listed on the preliminary ballot for SFWA's Nebula Award, and "The White Game" was nominated for the Short Mystery Fiction Society's Derringer Award.

His latest books are *Home Run Enchanted, Curveball Cursed*, and *Outfield Magicked*, which comprise the Fairies and Fastballs series, written with his daughter.

NEWSLETTER & CONTACT

Discover other work by Ron Collins at:
https://www.typosphere.com

Join Ron's Reader List, and get free books!:
https://typosphere.com/newsletter